A SAFE PLACE TO LAND

An Eastern Shore Romance

DEE ERNST

235
ALEXANDER
STREET

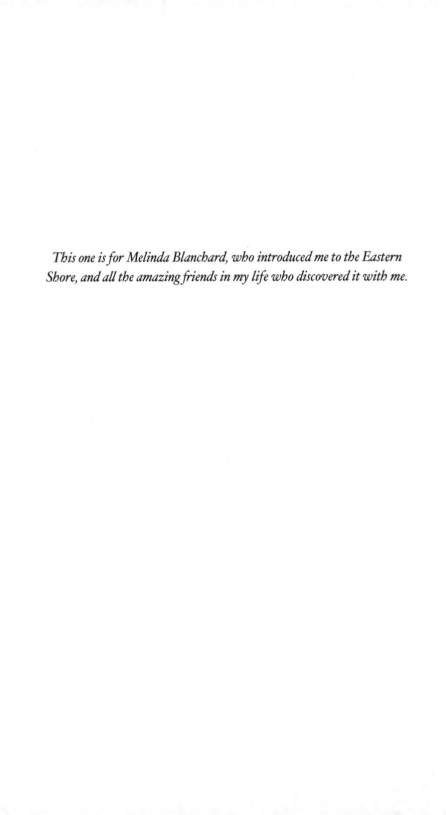

*This one is for Melinda Blanchard, who introduced me to the Eastern
Shore, and all the amazing friends in my life who discovered it with me.*

Also by Dee Ernst

Stealing Jason Wilde

Am I Zen Yet?

Better Than Your Dreams

A Slight Change of Plan

A Different Kind of Forever

Better Off Without Him

The Mt. Abrams Mysteries

A Mother's Day Murder

A Founders' Day Death

A Killer Halloween

A Deadly New Year

A Malicious Midwinter

A Fatal April Shower

The Eastern Shore Romances

A Safe Place to Land

Building Home

Chapter One

A single woman of a certain age on the Eastern Shore of Virginia was not what you would call a rare bird. In fact, there were so many of us in and around Cape Edwards that it was suggested we form our own official organization, complete with a clubhouse and a secret handshake. We joked about it, of course, and when Terri Coburn suggested we make the Edmonds' oldest son, a strapping young man who won the state wrestling championship, our official mascot, well, the idea really picked up some steam. But since we really didn't want to be single —or middle-aged—we chose not to make our status part of any official organization. Over the years we strengthened our friendships, watched some of us marry, embraced the newly single, and met once a week for breakfast at the Town Pharmacy.

Cape Edwards didn't have a CVS or a Rite-Aid, or even a Walgreens. We had the Town Pharmacy, right at the end of Main Street before you took the left to get onto State Road 31. Town Pharmacy was so much more than a mere drugstore. It sold cards, home accessories, candles, stockings, and oddly enough, Vera Bradley. There was also a luncheonette that served from six in the morning until two in the afternoon. I ate breakfast there, almost every Saturday morning, and had for almost fifteen years.

There were now five of us, as some of the original ladies from years back had moved on, one way or another. We met at eight thirty, sat at the same table, and pretty much ordered the same thing every week. Marie Wu sometimes asked for pancakes instead of her usual waffle, but our waitress, Wendy, was a quick young thing and never batted an eye.

It was at this breakfast table on an otherwise ordinary Saturday morning that I heard the news about Sam.

Stella Blount and I pulled into the parking lot at the same time from two different directions. Stella owned a shop of Main Street called Tidal Gifts, and during the summer season she made enough money to stay open for the other eight months of the year. She was short and round with hair cut in a short Afro with a patch of dark purple along one side. She was a shrewd businesswoman and a good friend.

"What's the word?" I asked as we met by the front door.

She shook her head. "There was something happening last night, but I don't know what it was. I imagine we'll find out in 3..2...1..."

Three faces looked up as we walked in, and I could tell by the looks that the something that had happened was bad.

"Should we be sitting down for this?" I asked.

Karen nodded her head and patted the empty seat next to her.

"Yes" she said. "You too, Stella."

Stella sat gingerly across from me. "Who died?" She said it lightly, sarcastically, but...

Terri took a deep breath. "It's Sam. He's gone. Last night, Charlie said. Heart attack." She reached across the table to grab my hand, holding it tightly. "I'm so sorry, Jenna."

They all watched, and I felt tears. "Damn," I muttered, and reached for a mug of coffee, poured in an excessive amount of sugar and stirred slowly with my free hand.

Sam had been my husband for almost five years. They had been the happiest and most miserable five years of my life. We were an unlikely couple to begin with. I'd been barely eighteen and had never been farther from Cape Edwards than Norfolk and Virginia Beach. Sam blew in from New York City and opened a bar on Main Street and hired me to waitress. He was forty at the time, traveled and experienced, had lots of money and a wicked sense of humor. We had what could best be described as a whirlwind courtship. My mother howled and complained and protested. She promised me trips to Europe and threatened to disown me. But I was in love, so Sam and I married, right there on the beach, both of us barefoot and a little high.

"Heart?" I asked.

Marie Wu nodded, her dark, bobbed hair dancing around her face. "Yep. Collapsed behind the bar. Glory and Charlie took turns doing CPR, but it was no use. By the time the EMTs got there, he was gone. I'm so sorry, honey."

I drank my coffee. We hadn't been very successful as a married couple, but for years we'd been the best of friends. "Well, that sucks." I'd been on Main Street last night. A headache kept me from staying late, but I'd had my usual beer with Sam around nine-thirty. He'd been fine.

Karen Helfman reached around me to give me a hug. She was older than I, just fifty, and was a yoga instructor. You wouldn't think there was much of a demand for yoga in a small town like Cape Edwards, but her studio was quite popular, drawing clients as far north as Exmore. She was very much into an all-natural way of living, so her hair was very gray and her face was wrinkled from too many walks in the summer sun. Her body was that of a twenty-year-old, but she looked sixty-five from the neck up.

"What are you going to do with the bar?" she asked.

I glanced around the table. They all leaned in expectantly.

Wendy came up to our table. She'd been working there for five years and knew us all too well. "The usual, ladies?" she asked.

Heads nodded around the table. I pushed my mug to the center.

"I over sugared this, Wendy. Sorry. Another cup?"

She nodded. "Sure, hon. I don't blame you, with losing Sam and all. We all know how much you still loved him," she said, and vanished.

"I didn't still love him," I muttered. I glanced up. All four faces showed perfect disbelief.

"Well, I didn't," I said louder.

"Then why the tears?" Marie asked. She was a tiny woman, Korean, and she was a lawyer up in Cheriton, specializing in property law. Property was a big deal on the Eastern Shore, and surveys had a tendency to be quite fluid and flexible things, keeping her quite busy.

"Look, we *all* loved him. He was my friend."

Terri reached across the table to grab my hand again and squeeze it. "Jenna, we all know why you never married again."

I pulled my hand back. "I never married again because there was no one around here worth marrying."

Marie clucked softly. "What about all those doctors across the Bay? Huh?"

I sighed. She was right, there had been plenty of doctors on the other side of the Chesapeake Bay Bridge, but most of them were already married. That hadn't kept me from sleeping with a few of them, but it really squelched any marrying plans.

"None of *you* remarried. Were you all in love with Sam?"

Terri shook her head. "Fifteen years is a long time to be without a man, Jenna."

I made a face. "And what makes you all think I've gone fifteen years without a man?"

The giggles erupted as Wendy brought my fresh mug of coffee. "What's the joke?" she asked.

"Jenna here was just about to tell a few tales out of school," Marie said with a smirk. "Apparently, she's been milking a few locals without us even knowing."

I waved my spoon. "No locals. I told you, this town is dry. But those doctors..."

4

More giggles, and Wendy joined in. "There's a new doc moving into the Booker place."

We all sat up. Wendy's mother was the realtor in town, and that made her a prime source of information.

"Married?" Stella asked.

Wendy shook her head. "Don't get too excited. A woman. Just her name on the paperwork, Mom said. She's planning to gut the whole house. She's got the McCann brothers to do the work."

Now, the McCann brothers were as close as Cape Edwards came to eligible bachelors, but they both worked so much that the women in town had a hard time getting them into any kind of social situation. Lord knows, enough of them had tried to get either of those boys, but it was hard to put the moves on a man when he was putting up sheetrock.

Terri raised her eyebrows. "Very useful information, Wendy. Thank you. When is she moving in?"

"Soon. Closing in a few weeks. Told Mom she's starting at the Riverside MedCenter first of the month." She glanced back at the kitchen. "I think you're up," she muttered, and moved away.

"Well now, *that's* good news," Karen said. "We could use another smart, successful woman in town."

"Maybe. But Jenna," Stella said. "What about Sam's place?"

"I don't know," I said slowly. "I never gave it much thought."

"Well, darlin', you were the only family he had, right?" Marie asked.

I nodded. "Yes. I mean, he never mentioned anyone except an aunt up in Long Island somewhere, so he may have cousins? But I guess I just never thought he'd actually die."

Karen snorted. "He was over sixty, drank like a fish and smoked those damn cigars. The only cardio he ever got was when he got worked up over a football game. I'm surprised he lasted this long."

"Oh, Karen, hush. I know exactly what Jenna means," Terri said. "Sam seemed...eternal." And she was right. He had boundless energy, charm, and a kind heart. He was a force. And now he was gone.

"Well, you have to keep it open," Stella said. "Sam's on Main is an institution now. I don't know what we'd do without it. And you know how popular it gets in the summer."

Wendy put our plates in front of us and disappeared, promising more coffee.

I stared at my eggs. Sam's had originally been a simple bar, dark and closed in. Sam had lived on the second floor when he first opened it, making, he said, for an easy commute.

When we married, we bought a house right on the Chesapeake Bay, a long, rambling brick affair on eight acres at the end of a road so twisted and rutted I always wanted to put up a sign that read, "Here There Be Dragons." It was there that Sam and I lived and loved and fought and loved some more until he left, went back to New York, and filed for divorce. I signed the papers, which gave me half the house and alimony for ten years.

The bar had remained shuttered until Sam made his reappearance two years later. By then, I'd finished college, had my nursing degree, and worked at a hospital across the bridge in Norfolk. I had stopped thinking he was the worst person in the world. It took a few months, but one night I walked back into his bar, ordered a beer, and we began the journey back to friendship.

Over the years the bar had grown. He'd bought the building next door when it had become vacant and added more windows and tables, and a kitchen. He went upward, breaking open the second floor and put in a balcony that ran around three sides. He still had his bachelor flat over the original place, two small rooms and a bath. He would joke that when he retired, he'd claim his half of the house and move back in with me.

"I guess the house is all mine now," I said slowly.

"I love your house," Stella said, dunking her toast in egg yolk. "A tough place to be in the weather, but it's just beautiful."

"But the bar, Jenna," Marie said. "You can't sell it."

I looked up. "Why not? I can't run it."

"Course you can," Karen said. "How hard can it be?"

"I have a job, remember?"

"But only three days a week," Stella pointed out.

"Three twelve-hour shifts a week," I corrected her. "And taking care of the house and the dogs and the garden, not to mention the goats...I don't have time to run a bar."

"You could quit nursing," Karen said. "Work right here in town. You've said for years now how you hate the commute over that dang bridge."

I sat back slowly. Quit my job? But I loved my job.

No, actually, I didn't. I'd just been doing it for so long I couldn't imagine doing anything else with my life.

"I guess I'll have to hear what Ellis has to say," I said, gratefully sipping my fresh coffee.

Terri rolled her eyes. "What do you think Ellis is going to say? The bar is yours, Jenna. And didn't you say you wanted to do something new and exciting now that you're the big four-oh?"

Forty is a big birthday. Ask anyone who's survived it. I'd spent the day alone, looking out over the Chesapeake Bay, trying to decide how I felt about being alive for so long. I'd thought about my work, my life, and about what I'd have done differently. I had also thought about what I'd want going forward.

The only definitive thing I'd decided was that I wanted a change. I didn't know what change, or how to go about that change, but I knew that was what I needed.

Sitting there, thinking about it, I thought that running Sam's on Main might be the answer.

I was still thinking about it when I got home. I shut off the car and sat, looking at the water, thinking about what it would mean to own Sam's on Main. Then I put my head down on the steering wheel and started to cry, and didn't stop until it seemed there were no tears left in the world.

The Sunday paper had an official death notice, saying nothing more than Sam Ferris had died of a heart attack on Friday evening, and that he was to be cremated, and that an official memorial service would be announced at a later time. Ellis Summer, the lawyer in town, had put the notice in the paper. Ellis spent a lot of his time doing that sort of thing. He was a family lawyer, which meant he took care of things that families in trouble or under duress forgot about doing.

Ellis Summer had an office on Main Street, right over the Grove Gallery. You had to walk up a narrow flight of stairs, perch on a landing so small you couldn't have more than two feet and the tip of an umbrella on it, and wait for Ellis unlock the door. He claimed he couldn't afford to have a stranger walk in while he was with a client. There was no waiting room or receptionist, no clerk slaving away in a dark corner office. There was just one long room with an ancient desk, a worktable, a wall of filing cabinets and a bookcase of law books.

Ellis had been in my class in high school. I'd known him all my life, and I knew he'd be a lawyer, just like his father, Eaton Summer. Eaton had handled my divorce, but as soon as Ellis passed the bar, he moved into his father's office, and Eaton Summer spent his retirement fishing and driving his poor wife crazy. They both died last year, within a week of each other.

I worked Mondays, Tuesdays and Wednesdays, but I called out for that Monday and rang Ellis first thing in the morning. He told me to come right over. I went up the stairs, knocked, and waited until he opened the door. He greeted me somberly, pointed to the familiar client chair, then settled behind his desk.

"Hey, Red," he said. Everyone I knew from high school called me Red, because I'd been the only person in the entire school with red hair. I'd hated the nickname, but over the years had accepted my fate. "I'm sorry about Sam. Thanks for coming by."

I nodded as I sat.

The file was right there in front of him. He opened it and cleared his throat. "I have his will," he began.

I nodded again. I'd learned years ago that to interrupt him for any reason only gave him the excuse to go back to the very beginning.

"Sam's wish was to be cremated immediately after his death. As executor of his estate, I've already instructed Kenny." Kenny was Kenny Malcolm, owner and operator of the Malcom Funeral Home, right in Cape Edwards.

"One year after his death, he wished to have a memorial service in the bar, with free food and drink for all, after which his ashes were to be taken out in Fred Harvey's boat and dumped in the Chesapeake Bay."

I took a breath. That sounded about right. "I wondered about that. He'd always said he didn't want a funeral. I was here to offer my help, but I guess I'm not needed?"

Ellis pushed up his glasses. "No, but thank you, Jenna. Around here we all still thought of you as a couple, albeit an unusual one. So I can understand your concern. I also appreciate the fact that you'd have expectations. However, Sam left everything to his son, Craig Ferris, of Chicago, Ill." He sat back. "Everything except for five thousand dollars to cover the cost of his cremation and the, ah, after party."

I opened my mouth, closed it, and sat up straight. What had Ellis just said? "Sam had a *son?*"

Ellis sighed and nodded. "Yes. Craig Ferris, born in New York. Mother was a Kelly Laslow, who died almost twenty years ago. My understanding was that Sam had a relationship with Kelly as a very young man, but did not know of Craig's existence until her death, at which time he became involved in his son's life."

"But wait...this was when we were still *married?*"

"The dates are very close. He may have filed for divorce at the same time he found out about Craig. He was not very forthcoming about that. But he told me that he and Craig had been in pretty much constant contact since then. Craig has been notified. I called him myself yesterday afternoon, and a certified letter has been sent."

I heard, quite clearly, the ticking of the grandfather clock that stood in the corner of Ellis' office. Sam had been one of the most important people in my life. I'd loved him and thought I'd known all there was to know about him. But he'd had a son, and for years he had kept that very important fact from me. How could he *do* that? But more than that...

"Ellis, you knew this and you never *told* me?"

He sat back, obviously shocked. "Jenna, Sam was my client."

"So was I."

"This was privileged information."

"Ellis Summer, we have known each other our whole lives. I introduced you to your wife, we've stood beside each other piling up sandbags to keep the Bay out of Main Street." I paused just long enough for a deep breath. "We saw each other naked in second grade."

He began to sputter. "Jenna, I'm a lawyer, and Sam was very clear about this. He felt very conflicted. He didn't want you to know, because he didn't want to hurt you. He knew how much you wanted children of your own, and well..." He waved his arms around. Ellis was short and skinny as a rail, and it was difficult, under the best of circumstances, for him to look like a person of authority. When he tried really hard, like right now, it was down-right comical.

"Ellis, you should be ashamed of yourself, sitting there trying to look all official when you've been lying to me for all this time."

He stood up and tried to exude authority. "It was Sam that lied to you, Jenna. He kept his lives very separate. Not only did no one around here know about his son, Craig had no idea Sam owned the bar. He knew very little about Sam's life in Cape Edwards." He tugged at the lapels of his suit, then sat back down again. "It was not my secret to share, Jenna. It was Sam's. And he chose not to."

I closed my eyes and sank back, feeling angry and betrayed. Sam and I had not just been husband and wife. We'd become the best of friends. Over all those years, he hadn't trusted me enough to tell me about his son, his own flesh and blood. I suddenly felt like I hadn't known the man at all.

I opened my eyes slowly. "Well. Yes." I looked around, picked up my purse from the floor, and glared at Ellis. "Well. Everyone

I've run into this past weekend told me that I needed to keep Sam's place open, and that I couldn't sell. Karen even suggested I quit nursing to run it. And you know what? I thought about it, even decided it was a good idea. I'm tired of twelve-hour shifts and that miserable commute over that damn bridge. I was looking forward to running the bar, fixing the menu, maybe even doing a little redecorating."

I stood up, feeling a little head of steam building up. "I was going to be on Main Street, Ellis. Join the Chamber of Commerce, maybe run for the Council. I'd be a person of influence in this town, maybe even the county, Ellis." I leaned across his desk. "I could have become the governor, Ellis, ever think about that? Governor of the whole Commonwealth. But no..." I shook my finger right up in his face. "No. And ya wanna know why? Because some stupid kid from Chicago is getting Sam's bar instead of me, that's why." I straightened. "At least I don't have to worry about any of *that* now, do I? I don't have to worry about the bar at all. It's Craig Ferris' problem now, right? Since he now owns Sam's on Main?"

Ellis stood. "Yes. But Jenna—"

I narrowed my eyes at him. "What Ellis? There can't be anything else to tell me that's going to top this."

He cleared his throat. "Craig inherits *everything*, Jenna."

It took a minute to sink in, and the bottom fell out of my stomach. "You mean...my house?"

Ellis cleared his throat again. "Not *your* house, Jenna. It's only half your house. The other half belongs to Craig Ferris."

"The hell it does," I roared.

Ellis actually staggered back, putting his arms out to balance himself. "No, really Jenna. He inherits Sam's half of the house." He cleared his throat. "You and Sam split everything, from the taxes to the new generator. Now, if you had taken over the fiscal responsibility of the property, then, well, maybe you'd have a case for taking the whole thing, but as it stands..."

I closed my eyes, remembering the conversations Sam and I

had about the house. He'd bought it outright and there had never been a mortgage. When we divorced, we split it fifty-fifty. As we had gotten older, I offered to buy him out, offered to pay all the taxes and insurance, and tried to wave off his payments to keep up the property. I thought he was being kind and generous.

"That snake," I growled. Ellis turned pale. "That miserable son of a bitch. It's a good thing he's dead, 'cause I swear, if I saw him right now, I'd strangle him with my bare hands."

Ellis sighed. "I'm sorry, Jenna."

"And I suppose you're on the side of this Craig person?"

"As executor, Jenna, I have to do all I can to carry out the terms of the will. It's my job, Jenna."

"Yeah? Well, well...you're a snake too, Ellis Summer."

I turned on my heels and stomped off, and my exit would have been quite impressive if not for the fact that the door was locked, and I had to fiddle with the damn thing for at least twenty seconds before opening it and slamming it, quite loudly, behind me.

The house that Sam Ferris and I shared hadn't changed much over the years. It had been brand new when we bought it, a typical eighties-style ranch with a huge fireplace in the living room, an expansive kitchen with enough room in the bay window for a long dining table, and what was called a split floorpan, the master suite on one side of the house, and three more bedrooms with two more baths on the other side. Sam and I had wanted children, and he was planning for the future. But in five years of pretty much nonstop sex, I'd never become pregnant.

Over the years, I'd rented the extra bedrooms out to various friends and newcomers to Cape Edwards. In the past few years they had remained empty, and I'd been thinking about them as potential Airbnb spaces. But I hadn't gotten around to the painting that was needed, and the bathrooms hadn't been spruced up since 2010. I lived quite comfortably in one half of the house, and for years it was more than enough. Now I saw the whole house as mine, and I wasn't about to let some idiot kid from Chicago come and take it away from me, not one square inch.

I pulled up by the front door, turned off the engine of the Grand Cherokee, and stared. The water surrounded me on three sides. Logan's Creek came in on the westernmost part of the property, spilling into the bay, which spread out before me so vast and blue it could have been an ocean. This was mine—the raised garden along the seawall, the trails going back into the woods, the enclosure along the drive where my six goats gamboled.

Mine.

I got out of the Jeep and slammed the door so hard that the dogs started barking. I stomped to the front door, threw it open wide, and stood back as they streamed out: Finn, a spry terror mix, Chloe, an aging Belgium shepherd, and Bit, a scrap of fluff so unidentifiable even my vet hadn't a clue what she actually was. They jumped around me in their usual style, as though I'd been gone three weeks instead of an hour, then ran off, sniffing.

I went into the house, stood in the center of the living room, and took several deep breaths. First things first. I needed a lawyer. I'd only used Ellis or his father for the whole of my life, and since Eaton was dead... I sat down and called Marie.

Her secretary put me through right away. "Hey, it's Jenna. So, Sam had a son that I never knew about. No one knew about him, I guess, except Ellis. This son has inherited everything, including Sam's half of the house. I need to know what I can do."

Marie whistled. "He had a son?"

"I know, right? I can't friggin' believe it. I don't know what he'll do with the bar, and I don't care. But what about my house?"

"Calm down, Jenna. It's easy. I'll get in touch with Ellis, get this person's address, and we'll make him a nice, reasonable offer. You have some savings, yes?"

I did. Working as a nurse hadn't meant a lot of money when I'd started, but after fifteen years, I made more than just a comfortable salary. And since my living expenses were low, I'd stashed quite a bit away in various bank accounts, stock funds, and bonds.

However. I was living in a four-bedroom house with eight acres of land, right on the Chesapeake Bay. Although I didn't know much about the real estate market, I had a feeling that waterfront property was going to have a hefty price tag.

"I have savings, Marie, but not enough to buy his half outright."

"So, you'll get a mortgage, Jenna. Do you want the house or not?"

"Yes."

"I'll get an appraiser out there, and we'll make an offer, and figure out the rest from there. He had a *son?*"

Bit came racing through the open front door and leapt on my lap. I scratched her ears. "Apparently this happened before he even moved down here the first time. The kid is now in Chicago."

"Well, that explains all those mysterious trips Sam used to take," Marie said.

I sat back. We all had joked about that for years. Every few months, Sam would take off for a long weekend, leaving Charlie in charge of the bar, and would return without so much as a word of explanation. At one point, Kenny Malcom had accused Sam of having a secret family down in Mexico, and Sam had run with it, telling wild stories of his common law wife and six kids who all lived in a shack on the beach in Baja. But the truth hadn't been that far off. He'd been visiting his son.

"God, you're right, Marie. I just can't believe he hid this from me for all these years. I mean, he used to talk to me about everything."

I heard her sigh. "We all have secrets, Jenna."

She was right. As much as I loved my girlfriends, and shared with them pretty much everything that happened to me, they would never know about the three years I'd spent sleeping with a married surgeon. And they never knew everything about Sam and I.

"I'll call Ellis right now, Jenna. Not to worry. You won't have to share your house with anyone, I promise."

I believed her. She wasn't just my friend. She drove a Mercedes and lived alone in a big, beautiful place right on the Seaside of the peninsula. A person didn't make that kind of money being a crappy lawyer.

I looked around my house. It needed really a good cleaning. For living alone, I was constantly amazed by how much crap I accumulated, and how big the dust bunnies grew. Having three dogs and a cat didn't help, but I long ago reconciled myself to the fact that the predominant accessory in my home would be pet hair.

I looked outside. Gray. Typical for early May. I could work in the garden. I had already put in a bunch of seeds: beans and beets, three different lettuces, melon, corn, squash... I'd been checking their progress religiously and watching the weather for a late frost, and I'd spent most of yesterday futzing around out there.

That left cleaning. I stood up, made a cup of tea, pulled an old Nora Roberts hardcover off of my bookshelf and settled in to read, Bit once again on my lap, Chloe and Finn at my feet.

I heard the pet door open and close, and Ghost, my gray cat jumped up to stretch out behind me on back of the couch.

It took a few minutes, but I finally relaxed enough to even get in a bit of a nap.

Chapter Two

❦

My usual shift ran from seven in the morning until seven at night. The dogs had their doggy-door, the goats were fed and watered, as well as milked, by my neighbor, Dave. In exchange, he used the milk to make his own brand of cheese that sold quite well in local markets. The garden had an automatic watering system. Being away from my house for more than half a day was no big deal, and although I was usually exhausted at the end of my working day, I was never to tired for DeeDee and Jack's, especially on Tuesdays, which was A Buck A Beer night. DeeDee and Jack's was a long gray building across from the Methodist Church, and it was right at the turn off the state highway on the way to my house. I passed it all the time. I didn't stop in *every* time, but some weeks, it was close.

It was the kind of place the locals knew, and the summer people drove right past. We shared lots of information with the tourists. After all, they brought in lots of money, and we who lived in the tip of the Delmarva Peninsula appreciated every penny. But we didn't talk to them about DeeDee and Jacks. Some things we just kept to ourselves.

When I pulled in that Tuesday night, still in my scrubs and

feeling stretched too tight from a hard day in the ER and my life in general, the parking lot was full. Well, not the parking lot, exactly, as that was a rather vague term when applied to DeeDee and Jack's. Parking area? Parking *field*? Whatever—I parked at the church and walked over. After all, I had the church's sticker on my back window, and I could just as easily have been the church itself, praying.

DD&J's was one long, narrow room, with an equally long, narrow bar, and behind that, a kitchen. No one knew what the kitchen looked like, which was just as well. When you consider that the linoleum-covered tables dated back to the sixties, and the recent hole in the floor had been repaired with a large sheet of reinforced steel just bolted into place, the condition of the kitchen was best left to the imagination. If the Health Department of the Commonwealth of Virginia thought it was good enough, well, the rest of us weren't going to argue.

The crowd on Tuesdays was always a little rough, but in one corner were familiar faces, and they waved me over as I came in.

Terri Coburn was there. Terri was our postmistress. At fifty, she had worked almost thirty years at the post office and had started to talk about retiring, but we all knew better. Terri lived for gossip, most of which she gathered at work, and she wasn't about to relinquish her advantage just because she was getting older. She scooted down the bench, making room for me to sit.

"Charlie says there's gonna be a new owner of Sam's on Main," she said. "What the heck is going on, Jenna?"

Charlie had worked for Sam since the bar had reopened years ago, and was Sam's bar manager. It was natural that Ellis would have told him what to expect.

DeeDee bustled over, set down my beer, and folded her arms under her bosom. "You know what's goin' on Jenna? 'Cause we here are all stumped. Who would Sam have given the bar to?"

I took a gulp of my beer, and it tasted just about perfect. "His son."

Silence fell. Seriously. The entire bar stopped talking.

I looked around. "And no, I didn't know a thing about it. Ellis could have knocked me over with a feather when he told me. Sam had a son. Craig Ferris, of Chicago. That's all I got."

Everyone started talking at once, and two beers and a burger later, I'd heard so many theories I could have written an entire book on the Secret Life of Sam Ferris.

I got up to go to the bathroom, one of the few spaces at DD&J's to have been rehabbed in the past twenty years, and as I was walking past the bar, Kenny Malcom reached out, grabbed me around the waist, and pulled me in close.

Now, Ken Malcom was a fairly attractive man, over six feet tall, broad shouldered and had a head of hair that would make Patrick Dempsey envious. Right after Sam left, and before Ken started dating his wife, Kate, he and I had gotten too drunk, flirted too much, and ended up in the gazebo right on the entrance to the beach, where we had such crazy sex that we both ended up with splinters in places too private to mention. It had never been repeated, but I'd thought about it. So, apparently, had he.

"Jenna, you are looking as sexy as ever," he murmured into my hair.

He was lying. I'd never been sexy. I was tall enough, but skinny as a rail. My most visible curve was the arch of my foot. No boobs, no butt and no hips made Jenna a very boring girl. My pale skin was covered with freckles. I'd admit that my hair was pretty spectacular, the exact color of slightly burnished copper, but it was hard to appreciate when it was pulled up on top of my head in a messy bun pretty much all the time.

I looked up at him. "Kenny, you and Kate having problems again?" Their marital spats were legendary, and rumor had it that Kenny spent half of his nights sleeping in the office of his funeral parlor.

"Now, Jenna, can't a man admire a beautiful woman without her thinking he's got an ulterior motive?"

"No," I said, and the guys standing at the bar all laughed. I pushed Kenny away and went back to sit beside Terri.

"Now, Jenna," she scolded. "Don't be mean to poor Kenny. You know Kate is a bitch."

"Then why did he marry her?" I grumbled, a question I'd been asking myself ever since he proposed to her.

Stella, at the end of the table, waggled her finger at me. "You're getting cranky in your old age, Jenna. You better watch out, or you'll end up a curmudgeon."

I made a noise. "Is that some big fancy word for a woman who don't take shit?"

The table laughed, but underneath, I cringed a little. I had noticed that my tolerance for anything even slightly less than perfect had waned. My life, I knew, had become smaller. With that came a smaller worldview. I didn't like that very much about myself but wasn't sure how to fix it. That was why the idea of owning Sam's on Main had struck such a chord. If I needed a place to restart my life, it would have been perfect.

Now, I had to find another second act. And in a small town like Cape Edwards, the options were very limited.

I left sooner than I wanted to. I didn't want to go back to my house. Not because I loved it less, but because I now knew that it could be taken from me, the one thing I thought was all mine. But if I stayed, there would a beer, another beer, and another after that, then someone would suggest a shot...

I had work the next morning and had to leave my house by five thirty. So I waved goodbye, drove home, and was asleep by ten.

My phone was always turned off during work, and all my friends knew it, so any calls I got from them went to voicemail and they never minded. However, the call from Marie the next day came in while I was on break, and luckily I took it right away.

"Jenna, I have an appraiser out at your place now but he's afraid to get out of the car. He says he's surrounded by a pack of dogs."

I sighed. When I was working, I opened up the larger pet door so that the dogs could get in and out of the house as needed. But...a pack?

"Marie, Bit is the size of a squirrel and Chloe has no teeth."

"True, but I know that Finn can be pretty loud. What do you want to do?"

I thought. "Tell him to wait. I'll call Dave next door. Dave can round up my savage pack and protect that poor appraiser from attack."

When I called Dave, he didn't believe me, then laughed hysterically, then said he'd run right over and put the dogs in the garden until the appraiser left. I went back to work and didn't think about it again. In fact, I didn't think about the appraisal until the following week, when, once again, Marie called. This time it went to voicemail, and when I listened, I almost had a heart attack.

"Jenna, babe, I sent that appraisal last week to Craig Ferris, and I just called this morning to follow up. He's not interested in selling, because as of noon today, he's in Cape Edwards. He was actually sitting in Ellis' office when he took my call, getting a key. He's intending to move in there today. I don't know what to do to stop him, Jenna. He was every legal right to half of that house. If you can get off work early, do it."

I pulled the phone from my ear and stared at it.

"Jenna, you okay?" another nurse asked.

I listened to the message again and immediately called Ellis.

I didn't even tell him who I was, but I'm guessing he knew right away. "Ellis, you miserable piece of crap, how dare you give that man the key to my house?" I'm not sure how loudly I was speaking, but I did notice that every single person in the break room turned to look at me.

"Jenna," Ellis said calmly. "We talked about this. Craig Ferris has every right to one half of the property. I could not, in good conscience, let him leave empty handed. He'd driven all the way from Chicago, and his children were with him."

I stood up slowly. "Children?"

"Three girls," Ellis said. "Very well behaved."

"You mean not only is a total stranger going to be living in my house, but now three screaming brats are coming too?" At this point, everyone in the break room had gotten comfortable. Someone may have actually had popcorn, or maybe not.

"They seemed well behaved," Ellis repeated, louder this time, as though it would make a difference. "Are you home now? They should be there fairly soon."

I looked around. I had never just left in the middle of a shift. This was the ER after all, and if I wasn't there, someone would notice. "I'm at work. But I'll try to leave as soon as I can."

"That's fine, Jenna. But remember, he has a legal right to be in that house. Don't, well..."

"Shoot him?" I asked. "Don't worry, Ellis, I'm going to save that for you." I shut off my phone, sat back down, and tried to take some deep breaths.

The jungle drums in a small hospital are the fastest means of communication ever. Before I could figure out what possible excuse I could give my supervisor, she was standing in front of me.

"What happened?"

I loved most of the people I worked with and considered many of them to be my friends, but they were work friends, and I didn't share much of my personal life with them. But they all knew about Sam and knew he had died.

I looked up. "Sam had a son, and in his will, he left everything to him, including his share of the house. The son is apparently on his way there now. To my house. With his kids."

It took her less than a second. "Go. We'll find cover. I know you're off tomorrow anyway, but if you need extra time for this, you've got it."

I fumed all the way out of the hospital parking lot. I fumed even harder midway over the bridge when I got another call from Ellis. I clicked on my Bluetooth.

"Jenna, Craig says he's afraid to get out of his car because of the dogs."

Good, I thought smugly. "Well, Ellis, I'm halfway over the bridge, so tell this Craig person I'm less than an hour away."

"Jenna, can't you get someone to go out there sooner? He's got three children with him."

"And they don't like dogs? Gee, that's going to be tough. How do they feel about cats, 'cause I have one of those, too."

He sighed. "You're not going to be gracious about this, are you?"

"Why should I be?"

"Jenna, it's not Craig's fault. This was all Sam's doing."

I clicked off my Bluetooth. Ellis was right. This was all Sam's fault. But Sam was dead, and I needed to be mad at someone, right?

Right?

There was a battered gray Suburban parked in front of my house. The windows were all open, and as I drove up, I could hear singing.

I wasn't much into kids' movies, but even I knew the sound-track from *Frozen* when I heard it.

Finn and Bit were sitting diligently on the front stoop. Chloe was sitting directly in front of the Suburban. All three pricked their ears when they saw me coming around the curve, and by the time I'd parked, they were all on my side of the Jeep, jumping and barking. At least today they had something to bark about.

I got out of the Jeep, scooped up Bit, and bent to give Chloe and Finn a few appreciative pats. Chloe may have been toothless, but she was big and had a deep, scary bark. Finn yapped, but looked pretty aggressive. I told them both to hush, then walked around the Jeep to confront Sam Ferris' son, who though he could just waltz in and take over half of my house, some snotty kid from the big city...

My only defense is that I'd never been good at math, plus, the shock of Sam's death and his having a son I never knew about *obvi-*

ously had me not thinking quite straight. Ellis said that Sam had a relationship with Kelly Laslow when he was young. So he probably fathered his son when he was in his, what, early twenties? Maybe even his late teens. When he met me, he was forty.

So that made Craig Ferris about my age. Almost the same age Sam had been when we first met. And Craig Ferris looked so much like his father I almost stopped breathing.

He got out of the Suburban slowly. He was built like Sam, slope-shouldered but with a broad, muscular chest. His dark blond hair was already starting to thin on top, just like Sam's had, and he had big brown eyes and a wide, lazy mouth. He held out his hand, and I shook it automatically, still staring at his face. Those were Sam's cheekbones, all right, and the same jaw...good God, was that really a dimple in his chin deep enough to take a warm bubble bath in?

"I'm Craig. Pleased to meet you, Jenna. This is awkward. I'm sorry."

I withdrew my hand and took a breath. "You look just like him," I whispered.

He shrugged. "Yeah. Kinda weird, I guess." He looked down at Chloe, sitting at my side, her upper lip curled and a low rumble in her throat. "Will your dogs eat any of my kids?" he asked.

"What? No. She has no teeth. And Finn here will just grab the cuff of your jeans and tug until you play with him."

I looked past him into the Suburban. A young girl got out, tall and skinny, maybe twelve or thirteen. And out of the back poured two little girls, with identical faces, both wearing jeans and plain red t-shirts.

"Are those your goats?" asked one.

"What's your dog's name?" asked the other

"Can we fish here?"

"Do you have a pony?"

"Do we have to go to school?"

"Is there a bus?"

"Can we get a boat?"

23

"Girls?" Craig called out. "Manners."

One of the twins came up to me. "I'm Maddie. This is Larissa. You can tell us apart because I have a freckle on my nose and she doesn't. Can I pet your dog? Please?"

I held Bit out to her. The little girl leaned over close enough for their noses to touch. Bit started to wriggle with happiness, so I pushed her into Maddie's arms. "That's Bit. She likes you. But be careful, she'll steal the food right off your plate."

The two girls were tiny, and had big brown eyes like their father, cute pug noses and pink rosebud lips, and long, blondish hair in matching pigtails. Seriously? They couldn't have mean expressions and really bad teeth? They couldn't be animal haters? They had to be adorable urchins?

The older girl came around the Suburban and stuck out her hand. "Amanda. Hi." Her face was thin and sad, her eyes small with dark smudges beneath.

I shook her hand. "Jenna Ferris."

"Are you our grandma?" Larissa asked. She'd come up beside her sister, and Bit was frantically licking the side of her face.

"No," I said, rather too loudly. "I am nobody's grandma."

"But," she went on reasonably, "you were married to Grandpa Sam."

"True," I said. "But I had nothing to do with your dad, here. In fact," I said, looking straight into Craig's big brown eyes, "I didn't even know he existed."

Craig cleared his throat. "Do you think, maybe, we could go inside?"

Plan A had been, if he asked that question, to say no. That was before he was tall and drop-dead gorgeous with twin cherubs and a teen with such sad eyes. I pushed my way past him and unlocked the front door.

The dogs all rushed in from behind me, and Larissa and Maddie ran all the way from the front door to the big picture window overlooking the Bay. Craig let out a low whistle.

"That's some view," he said.

I nodded. "Yep. I get some amazing sunsets. Uh, listen, I really didn't expect you to just show up here."

I looked up at him. He was obviously uncomfortable. "Yeah. Well, we left Chicago in sort of a hurry."

Larissa had wandered into the kitchen, Maddie right behind her. I tried to remember if I'd let any food on the counter or dishes in the sink...

"Grandpa Rob was coming after us," Amanda said, sinking into the couch and stretching her legs out, propping her feet on the coffee table.

"Feet off the table," Craig said immediately. She threw him a look of absolute disgust and dropped her feet to the floor.

I put my feet up there all the time but knew this wasn't the time to mention that. "Coming after you?"

Craig ran his fingers through his hair, and then tugged at the ends. A Sam move. "It's complicated. The thing is, we're here because we have no place else to live, and my girls need a roof over their heads. This house is huge, so I'm sure there are a few rooms we can move into until we get a more, ah, formal arrangement."

Well.

Craig Ferris looked so much like his father had looked when we first married that all sorts of long, forgotten feelings came rushing back. I hadn't been a virgin when I first met Sam, but compared to the boys I'd slept with before, he'd been a revelation. Sex between us had been so hot that we stayed together for that reason alone, long after everything else we thought we shared had fallen apart. And looking at Craig, those shoulders, the strength in his arms, well...whatever. I was thrown off balance. Big time.

But he wasn't. Looking at me obviously didn't evoke anything, and he was all business.

"Sure," I said. "Come on this way."

Maddie and Larissa had already made their way to the far side of the house, and were in the room with the twin beds. Maddie was jumping on one, and Larissa was looking into the closet critically.

"Stop," Craig said, and Maddie immediately hopped off the bed. If nothing else, he had them well trained.

"So, I guess this could belong to the two of you," I said. "What do you think?" I hadn't been in any of these rooms in a while, and had almost forgotten what they looked like. This one was pretty grim. The color of the walls looked like wrinkled elephant skin and the carpet seemed to be growing stuff out of it.

Larissa opened one of the dresser drawers. I could see old shelf paper, faded and browned. "We need another dresser," she said. "And the closet needs fixed. And the walls?" She looked up at Craig. "Pink?"

He nodded, and ruffled her hair. "Whatever color you want."

He peeked into the hall bathroom. Entirely beige. "At least there's a tub," he muttered. The next bedroom was brighter, and had a small, private bath attached. "Amanda," he said. The final bedroom was dark and narrow, no curtains or a bedspread.

"Guess you don't really use these rooms much, do you?" he asked.

I shook my head. "No. I live pretty much on the other side. Sam had wanted a big house because he always thought there'd be a ton of kids living here." I stopped. I guess now there were.

Craig walked back and called to his girls. I sat and watched as they carried in suitcases. Maddie made a second trip for a clothes-basket full of stuffed animals.

Bit followed her down the hall. Finn jumped up on my lap and looked confused. "Yeah, buddy, I know," I told him. "We have something of a roommate conundrum."

He whimpered and tried to snuggle in closer.

"No, I don't know how long they'll be here."

Chloe, came up and put her giant head on my knee.

"Yes, Bit is acting like a traitor, but you know how he feels about shiny new things."

I felt Ghost jump up behind me. My family watched as Sam's family carried more things into the house.

I kept repeating, *this is not his fault, this is not his fault*. This man had absolutely nothing to do with the situation we were both in. He was obviously under pressure to find a safe place for his kids, and I was sure that once things calmed down, we would reach a nice, sensible agreement, and he would get the hell out of my house.

Finally, Craig came into the living room. He stared down at me, and I thought how I must have looked to him, in wrinkled scrubs, my hair pulled up and looking like a rats nest, surrounded by animals.

"No reflection on your housekeeping skills, but is there a vacuum cleaner we could use?"

"Yes, as a matter of fact."

"Good. And some spray cleaner? And lots of paper towels?"

I should have felt embarrassed, but I didn't. If he was going to just move into a person's home with no warning, then he could do his own cleanup.

"Done."

"We should probably go to the grocery store," he said. "They're going to be hungry pretty soon."

I took a breath. "Well you're going to hit traffic right now. I have juice in the fridge, a rotisserie chicken, frozen green beans, and an apple pie, if you think that can hold them until tomorrow. I only work Monday, Tuesday and Wednesday, so I'll be happy to show you around tomorrow. I guess you have to get them in school?"

He nodded.

I sighed. "I really don't want you here, Craig. I can't even imagine how this is going to work. But until we figure something else out, I can't throw you and your girls out in the street. In fact, even if I could, I probably wouldn't."

He nodded thoughtfully. "Well, at least you're honest. Yeah, this sucks for me, too. I wouldn't be here if I had another choice." He narrowed his eyes. "I thought you'd be way older. You know, Sam's wife."

I smiled back. "And I thought you'd be younger. Sam's kid."

"He was something else, my dad."

"I thought I knew him. I thought he was my friend."

"He was my *father*."

We looked at each other for a few seconds.

"Well," I finally said, "it looked like he lied to us both."

"That's one thing we have in common, I guess."

"Yeah."

We looked at each other for a bit more, then he shrugged and left.

I texted Stella, Karen Marie and Terri for an emergency beer at DeeDee and Jacks.

I got there first and snagged a booth. DeeDee practically ran over to me.

"Was that Sam's son in town today? Melanie said he looked just like him."

I nodded. "Yep, he's here. With three daughters. Right now, they're watching Jeopardy in my living room while my dogs are locked up in the laundry room. Bit's fine, but Finn is being a real stinker."

"Oh, Jenna, what are you going to do?"

"Hope they win the lottery." I looked up as Stella and Terri came in together. Terri was still in her work clothes, black pants and a polo shirt with US Post Office embroidered on the pocket. Her gray-blond hair was straight and cut in a short bob, and her blue eyes were wide as saucers.

She slid in beside me. "What is going *on?*"

I looked up at DeeDee. "Just bring a pitcher, Dee, and glasses. We may be here a while."

Dee shook her finger at me. "Don't talk about nothin' important without me," she said before darting off.

Stella sat across from me. "I hear he's the image of Sam," she said.

I nodded. "Yes. But not the sixty-something-year-old, gosh-if-he-had-hair-and-no-paunch Sam. Remember Sam when we were first married? And he was tall and good looking and we couldn't keep our hands off each other? Well, *that's* what Craig looks like."

Stella sat back. "Oh, my."

DeeDee set a pitcher in front of us and poured. "I do remember Sam when he first got here. Every single woman in the county wanted him. Lots of married women too. He was a looker, that boy."

I drank down my beer in a long gulp. "He's tall like Sam, too. With broad shoulders...I gotta say ladies, it brought back a whole lotta memories."

Karen came scurrying through the door and pulled up a chair. "Thanks," she said, taking a glass from Dee. "What did I miss?"

"Jenna here has the hots for Sam's kid," Terri said.

"No, I do not," I shot back. "And he's not a kid. He's close to forty. Maybe over forty."

"But," Stella said. "He is hot."

I nodded. "Oh, yes. And he has three girls."

Marie came in last, sitting down next to Karen and looking up at Dee. "Aren't you working?" she asked.

DeeDee shook her head. ""They all can get their own beer. I wanna hear this. Three girls?"

"Yes. Twins, maybe five or six, who look like...moppets, with big eyes and rosy cheeks and friggin pigtails." I drained my glass and held it out while DeeDee poured another. "They're so damn cute all they need is a mop and pail to be in the chorus of *Annie*."

"So he's *married* and hot?" Terri asked.

I stopped drinking and set my glass down slowly. "I don't know."

"I do," Marie said. "He told me his wife died last year, and that's why he was coming here in the first place. He said he needed a fresh start."

"He also said he left Chicago in a hurry," I told them. "And Amanda said her grandpa was after them."

"Amanda the moppet?" Stella asked.

I shook my head. "No, Amanda the tragic teen."

"Well, of course she's tragic," Karen said. "Her mother *died*."

I pushed aside my beer glass and dropped my head onto the table, my forehead settling right into the wet ring of condensation. "I just want them to go away and leave me alone," I wailed. "But he's gorgeous and the twins are too adorable and Amanda is grieving because their *mother* died." I lifted my head. "What am I going to do?" I asked them all.

DeeDee sniffed. "Well, Jenna, you might try to do something with your hair. It's your best feature, and it's always tied up in that knot on top of your head."

Terri folded her hands together. "You cannot be hateful to little girls."

Stella nodded. "That's right."

Karen nodded thoughtfully. "Maybe a haircut? Some layers would do wonders. And you might try a padded bra? If you're going to be comforting, you should also look soft and roundish, you know?"

I rolled my eyes. "No. I do not know."

Marie sipped her beer delicately. "Jenna, you've got a man here who's going to be running Sam's on Main, which is a big deal, and he's good looking *and* a widow. Every single woman in fifty miles is going to be on Craig Ferris like white on rice, and he's living in *your* house. Wear a little lipstick, girl. At least try."

"But...oh, God." I put my head down again. "What if he's a miserable prick?"

I heard Stella sigh. "Then you can just pass him on to someone else."

I lifted my head. "Can someone drive me?" I asked.

Terri nodded. "Me and Stella can tag team."

"Good," I said. I looked at DeeDee. "A shot. Tequila. Make it two."

Chapter Three

When I woke up, the sun was barely peeking over the water, and my room was bright. I hadn't managed to draw the drapes before I got into bed the night before. I was surprised to see I'd managed to take off my shoes.

All three dogs were in bed with me, and I eased out slowly. Only Chloe woke, lifting her head, sniffing, then going back to sleep. It was too early for them. On my days off, they slept in later than I. Smart dogs.

I pulled off my clothes from the night before, changed into sweatpants and my prized *Star Wars* T-shirt, and padded out to the kitchen in my bare feet. I made coffee, then sat at the long, narrow table that was pushed up against the bay window, overlooking my yard and the Bay. I cracked open a window and cool, damp air rushed in. It also let in the sound of the birds quarreling in the trees.

"You came in late last night?" Craig said behind me.

He was standing, wearing pajama bottoms of faded gray, snug around his hips, and a black T-shirt. I swear I could see every friggin' muscle in his chest. I closed my eyes and wondered why I hadn't at least *tried* to find a slinky black nightgown to wear to get my morning coffee.

"Um...yeah. Had a few with some friends. They drove me home. Late." I wanted to mention, just for conversation sake, that my tongue still felt like the bottom of a litter box, but decided against it.

"Can I have some coffee?"

I waved my mug. "Sure. Cream is in the fridge. You all get to sleep okay last night?"

I heard him stirring, the soft clink of a spoon against the sides of the mug. "I couldn't find any sheets for my bed."

"Oh. There's an extra set in the top of your closet."

"The closet is full of boxes."

Right. That was where all the old Christmas decorations I didn't know what else to do with had been stashed. "I'll empty that out today, and find those sheets."

"Thanks."

He sat on the other side of the table, and we looked at each other. I was fairly sure he hadn't slept well. How could he? New place, dogs barking to be let out, girls probably all upset. But I knew that, side-by-side, he'd win hands-down any early morning beauty contest.

I cleared my throat. "So, tell me why you don't have any place else to live." That was, I thought, a relevant question. After all, the answer was why he was in my house in the first place.

He ran his hands over his face. "My wife and I were in the middle of a pretty ugly divorce when she...died. Car accident. She was impaired." He paused. "I'd had a bit of a problem with that myself. I'm sober now for eight years, but she tried to use it to get full custody of the girls."

"Wait. You're an alcoholic, and you're going to be running a *bar?*"

He shrugged. "Until I find a buyer, yes. It's all I've got. I spent whatever savings I had on lawyers, and I don't think the employment opportunities for a web developer are all that great in Cape Edwards."

"You could probably find something across the Bay," I told him.

"And I'll look there. Once things have settled down." He stared down into his mug.

"So, why don't you have any other place to live?"

"Because the house we'd been living in belonged to Deb's—my wife's—father. And he's taken up the fight for custody of the girls. So I had to leave in a hurry. If I hadn't gotten that call from Ellis Summer, I don't know what I would have done." He took a long gulp of coffee, looked at me, and shrugged briefly.

We sat. "I'm sorry about Sam," I said at last. "Were you guys close? Ellis said he'd been in contact with you for a while."

He shrugged again. "Sam didn't come into my life until I was an adult. He didn't even know I was alive until Mom died. But when he found out, boy, he really did try. I mean he wanted to be a father, you know? Christ, the first thing he did when we met was take me to a baseball game. I was almost twenty-five years old, and he wanted to take me to a ball game." He shook his head. "He was a great guy, he really was. Treated me and my girls like gold."

Yes, I imagined that Sam would. He'd wanted to be a father. He used to joke that was why he'd married me, because I was young enough to have a dozen kids for him, and I think there was a grain of truth there.

I did some quick math in my head. It wasn't my strongest suit, but even I could subtract. He was twenty-five when Sam came into his life. That was right when Sam left me and went to New York. I was twenty-three. "You're older than me? Forty-two?"

He nodded. "Yeah. How old are you?"

"Forty." It all made sense now. That was why he went back to New York and filed for divorce. A son. He'd finally gotten what he'd always wanted and putting up with a crazy girl like me wasn't worth it any more.

"He found out about you and filed for divorce," I muttered.

"Oh, God, I'm sorry," Craig said, looking stricken.

I put my hands up. "No, no, please, Craig, don't think it was all because of you. Sam and I were pretty much over by then. In fact, the only time we were even civil to each other—" I stopped. What was the protocol for telling a man that the only time a woman was civil to his father was when they were having sex? I dropped my eyes.

If he wanted to hear the end of that sentence, he hid it well. "What broke you up?"

"I was young and stupid and he wasn't," I said, which was the truth. After working at the bar for two years, I went off to college, and for the first time saw what life was like outside of Cape Edwards. I wanted to go to keg parties and lectures by Carl Sagan. My husband wanted a wife who made him dinner and massaged his back—and front. I didn't understand what a twenty-plus-year-age gap meant. Maybe I didn't want to understand. "We became good friends after he came back," I told him. "But he never told me about you."

He looked at me evenly. "He never told me about you, either. He never talked about this place at all, what he did, the people he knew. I stopped pressing. If he wanted his secrets, then fine. He was entitled to secrets." He took in a deep breath, held it, then let it to out slowly. "Listen, Jenna, my girls and I have had a really tough year. I'm here because I needed a safe place to land, you know? I'll sell the bar, get a job, and let you buy me out. I just need some quiet, stable time with my girls so we can all feel like a family again. Okay?"

What choice did I have? Here was this obviously nice man in a crappy position. I could be a total bitch or a decent human being.

"Okay." I pushed away from the table. "I need to shower and wash the smell of beer off my skin. When the kids are up, we'll go into town for breakfast. I'll show you the Food Lion, where the schools are, and maybe you can take the girls out to the beach for a bit. Supposed to be warm today. Besides, the whole town is dying to get a look at you all."

He ran his hand through his hair. "That sounds good. Thanks.

But Jenna...I'd appreciate it if you kinda kept the details to your-self. I owe you an honest explanation of what's going on, but I don't want the gossip to start before I even clock in my first week."

I nodded. "Yeah, I hear you. The jungle drums around here are vicious. Your story is yours to tell, Craig."

I brought my coffee mug to the sink and left him quietly sitting, staring as the sun came up over the Chesapeake Bay.

We had breakfast at Shorty's.

During the summer, there was a line pretty much all the time outside Shorty's. Breakfast, lunch, dinner, after dinner...people were willing to wait. Early May meant only the locals, so although the tables were close to full, we walked in and sat right down at the big table by the window. The conversation didn't actually stop when we came in, but there was a noticeable lull, then rise. Sam's family was getting its first official introduction to Cape Edwards.

"Morning, Elise," I said as the waitress passed out menus. "This is Craig Ferris, Sam's son. Craig, Elise runs the front of the house here, so if you want a seat during season, start sending her flowers and chocolates now."

Craig looked up. "Pleasure, Elise. Jenna here talked you up all the way over."

Elise looked pleased. "Makes sense if she did. She's one of our favorite customers. Coffee for two? And what do the young ladies want to drink?"

Amanda sunk down a bit in her seat. "Hot tea?"

Craig opened his menu. "Milk for the other two, thanks."

Elise nodded and trotted off.

Craig looked carefully at the menu. "What do you think? Jenna seemed to think that waffles are the way to go. Her description was quite...convincing." He was being kind. I talked about those waffles the whole trip over.

Maddie nodded as she bounced in her seat. "Yes, please. One

really big waffle with lots of bananas and chocolate syrup all over the top."

"Ah, no," Craig said.

Larissa opened the menu and seemed to look at the items very carefully. "What's a c-r-e-p-e?"

"A really thin pancake," I explained. "And it's usually rolled up around fruit."

She considered. "Does it come with whipped cream?"

"No," said Craig. "It doesn't come with chocolate syrup either. Remember what we said about morning food and snack food?"

Maddie and Larissa looked at each other, gave identical eye rolls, and sighed.

"Can I have a crepe? With whipped cream?" Amanda asked.

Craig stared at her. "Really? Amanda? Can you not even *guess* the answer?"

Maddie and Larissa giggled at the exact same time.

"So...that's a no?" Amanda asked, perfectly innocent.

"That's a no."

The twins, to their credit, did not stick out their tongues, make faces, or otherwise attempt to make a statement.

Elise came back with a tray, distributed her goods, and quickly took orders. Craig ordered eggs and toast. Very boring, considering all the other options. I stuck to my usual order, maple-nut pancakes with homemade sausage. The girls all went for the waffle.

Amanda spent about three minutes dunking her tea bag in and out of her mug, during which time Maddie and Larissa asked thirty-seven questions about Shorty's. I had most of the answers. I recognized pretty much all of the people at the other tables and made eye contact or smiled at most of them. No one pulled up a chair to ask Craig what his intentions were, but that may have been because of the kids at the table.

Craig finally held up a hand to silence the twins. "So, Jenna, first I think we need to get these girls into school, yes?"

Maddie and Larissa both sighed.

"School is stupid."

"They can never tell us apart."

"Will we have to wear name tags?"

"Maybe I can have blue hair instead of blond like Maddie?"

He held up a hand again. "Stop. Jenna?"

"Well, the elementary school is close. Amanda will have to go up to Eastville for middle school. They can all get a bus, but I doubt you'll get a pickup close to the house. You'll probably have to take them out to the main road."

"That's not a problem."

He was wearing a denim shirt, faded and stretched across his shoulders. He hadn't shaved, so there was a faint stubble coming in a reddish-gold. He drank some coffee. "That Summer guy gave me keys to the bar, but I didn't actually go in yesterday."

Ah. "I'll be happy to go with you, introduce you. Glory, the cook, is usually there by ten. We could stop there first, if you like."

Maddie started bouncing again. "I wanna see Grandpa's bar," she said, rather loudly. If there was any one person in Shorty's who was wondering who I was having breakfast with, she probably answered the question.

Craig tilted his head at her. "You know that little girls aren't supposed to be in bars," he said.

Maddie continued bouncing, undeterred. "But it's *our* bar," she said. "I can be there if I want."

Olivia Kopecknie materialized so quickly I wondered if she'd been hiding under the floorboards and just rose up at Craig's side. "Jenna, honey, aren't you going to introduce me?"

Olivia and I had hated each other all through elementary school, middle school, high school, and she had not been invited to my wedding. For some reason, she was always competing with me. She liked to tell people she had better grades in high school, got out of college sooner than I did, had a job at a better hospital... would even point out that her Jeep was newer than mine. She was definitely ahead in the husband department, three to my one. She was curvy and quite pretty with bottle-blond hair and lots of mascara. This morning she was dressed in jeans so tight I could almost see the cellulite on her thighs through the denim.

"Olivia, this is Craig Ferris and his daughters, Amanda, Maddie and Larissa."

She practically reached over and took Craig's hand off his coffee cup. "Olivia Wheaton," she murmured.

"Oh? Which husband's name is that again?" I asked.

She ignored me. "I'm so sad about your father. Sam was a pillar of the community and will be missed." She managed to say all those words and sound completely sincere while never moving her bright red lips.

Elise came up behind her. "Olivia, you've got to move or pass around these plates," she said.

Olivia stepped to the side and Elise served us. As soon as the plates hit the table, Olivia moved in again.

Craig nodded politely. "Thank you, Olivia."

She crouched down next to him. "I heard that you just came down from Chicago," she purred. "Where are you staying here in Cape Edwards?"

"He's staying with me, Olivia. At the house." I smiled brightly, then bent to smother my pancakes with syrup.

She cracked a little. "Oh?"

Craig picked up his fork, but she didn't take the hint, so he put it back down. "Yes. We're all camped out there right now. One big, happy family."

She glanced around the table. "Oh?"

Amanda was helping Maddie cut up her waffle, and I turned to help Larissa.

"Jenna has goats and dogs and a big garden," Maddie said.

"And the house is really big," Larissa said.

"We're going to paint our bedroom pink."

"And get a new dresser."

"There's a big TV and we have lots of movies."

"The bathroom is gross but I saw boats out on the water this morning."

I finished with Larissa and went back to my own breakfast. "See, Olivia? One big, happy family."

She stood abruptly, and I inwardly sighed. Now, aside from the detailed description of every single thing we all ate for breakfast racing around town, word would be that Craig and I were already shacking up. But the look on Olivia's face almost made it worthwhile.

"Well," she said, "I'll let you all get on with your breakfast. Nice meeting you." She laid a hand on Craig's shoulder. "I hope to see much more of you."

Slut. Even though she was already imagining Craig and I as a couple, she wasn't above making a move on him anyway. I kept my head down and kept on eating.

Amanda had been eating her waffle in tiny bites. I glanced at her. "Like it?"

She nodded and leaned over to me. "Who *was* she?"

"Do you know what a nemesis is?" I said in as quiet a voice as possible. The last thing I needed was Maddie bouncing up and down, shouting nemesis at the top of her lungs.

Amanda frowned, then smiled shyly. "I get it. What a bitch."

Craig, who must have had hearing like a hound dog, looked up sharply.

I smiled at him sweetly. "Amanda here was just making a very astute observation."

He looked from Amanda back to me, stone faced. "I can imagine."

Luckily, the twins couldn't talk and eat at the same time, so the rest of the meal was fairly peaceful. I paid the check, waved happily at Olivia on the way out, and we all turned down Main Street away from Sam's on Main.

Cape Edwards was built on a grid. Main Street ran east to west, fronting the marina. Behind it were tree-lined streets of mostly brick homes built by the Cape Edwards elite back at the turn of the century. Front Street was at the west end and ran all the way along the Bay beach. Homes there were newer, built for summer visitors.

The tour was, therefore, fairly short. We walked up to the water, and the twins jumped and whined and pleaded, but to no avail. Beach time would be another day. Then we walked in the opposite direction, past the well-established storefronts, as well as a few newcomers to our little commercial district. There, just across from the entrance to the marina, stood Sam's on Main.

The door was open even though the sign said Closed. I felt a rush of emotion as I pushed my way in. I'd spent so many nights here, before and after Sam and I had married. This was the hub of social life in Cape Edwards. The old-timers all had their places at the bar. The dartboard had never been replaced. The leather that topped the stools was cracked and soft as butter. In the newer restaurant section, square tables and mismatched chairs could be pushed together for impromptu poker games after hours. The air smelled of tobacco. Not cigarette smoke, but the tobacco from Sam's cigars. He'd quit smoking years ago, and, it was illegal to smoke anything in the bar, but it filtered down from his place upstairs.

"Glory?" I yelled. The twins ran past me and both scrambled to climb up on the stools by the bar. Craig stood in the doorway, looking around, an odd expression on his face.

Glory Rambeau lumbered in from the back. She was African-American, almost six feet tall, had stupendous breasts and several stomachs. She'd been cooking for Sam for almost twelve years, and just by looking at her you knew that her food was all southern comfort. It was, too, but with a contemporary edge that had gotten the restaurant consistently excellent reviews as far as Norfolk and Virginia Beach.

She swept me into her arms and hugged me, lifting me up off the floor. When she dropped me and stepped back, her eyes were wet. "Damn him anyway," she mumbled. "Damn that man, dying like that, without a word of warning. Why couldn't he get sick and pine away like a normal person?"

I shook my head. "I wish I could tell you, Glory. This is his son, Craig."

She narrowed her eyes and walked toward him.

"You sure enough look like your daddy," she said. She put her fists on her hips. "What are you planning, son? I gotta know because summer's coming and things have to start happening."

Craig came closer. "What things?"

"We need to hire more help for one thing. In the next few weeks, we need to be taking on three more waitresses at least. Sam already hired them, way back in February, and they're all girls who worked here last year, but they need retraining. Are you going to work the bar? Because if not, you need another bartender fast. Two maybe, 'cause Charlie's been drunk since your daddy died and poor Mark's been doing double time. And one of our suppliers over at the docks needs a talking to or we won't be getting the fresh fish we need when we need it, and I am *not* going to go through that again."

Glory got her training in San Francisco and had worked in some pretty high-class restaurants. Born in Boston with no tolerance for fools, she'd been Sam's right hand woman and had loved Sam's on Main as much as he did.

Craig cleared his throat and looked past her, where Maddie and Larissa had climbed down from their stool and were now actually behind the bar. Amanda had been looking at all the framed posters on the wall, but turned and darted after her sisters.

"I will have these three in school by next week," he said. "Make a list of what we need to talk about. Here's the thing, Glory." He stepped even closer. They were almost eye to eye. "I'm an alcoholic. I need to be on the restaurant side. And I'm not planning on keeping the place. I'm an IT guy. I program computers. I know nothing about food or bars or business. But I will do whatever you tell me to do to keep this place just as it was until somebody who knows what the hell they're doing can take over."

Glory scowled at him, then glared at me, even though nothing here was my fault.

I held up both hands. "What can I say, Glory?"

She took a deep breath, expanding her already impressive chest by at least a foot. "Well, at least you're honest, and you don't look like a complete idiot. We can make it through the weekend. I know what we need, we all know what we have to do." She stuck her finger in his face and shook it. "Don't go selling this place without letting me have the first crack, you hear? When you decide that's what you want to do, you come to me before anyone else."

I'd seen Sam crumble when confronted by Glory and her finger, but Craig seemed to be made of sterner stuff. "Got it."

She turned and marched back into the kitchen.

Craig turned, looking around at the bar, then walked into the dining room. He glanced up at the open balcony. "Does this get filled every night?" he asked.

I followed him in. "During the season, yes. In the winter, there are a few book clubs that meet up there, and a bunch of women play mahjong on Tuesdays. This is a popular place. There's music four nights a week in season, and Sam had started a comedy night that he was pleased with." My eyes filled with tears at the memory of the first comedy night, a night in late September two years ago, when a very drunk Cody Wylie, a local fisherman, premiered his stand-up act, skewering the regulars, and keeping us all in stitches. Sam had been in rare form that night and promised Cody a regular slot. Then he and I had gone upstairs and made love on his rumpled king-sized bed. We'd done that over the years, Sam and I, when we felt particularly happy about something. Or sad.

That had been the last time we shared that bed.

I cleared my throat. "You keep looking around like you've been here before."

Craig ran his hands over his face slowly. "They met in a bar, you know, my parents. My mom's family ran a little tavern in Brooklyn, a tiny neighborhood place. It looked just like this."

"All bars look alike," I said.

He shook his head. Maddie had clamped on to his leg and he lifted her, balancing her on his hip as he walked back into the bar. "Not all bars look like this," he said. "He made this to look just like Mom's place."

I opened my mouth to argue with him, then stopped, because he was right. Sam's on Main *didn't* look like other bars. Sure, maybe the high tin ceilings, and the bar itself—well, long and wooden was pretty much standard, right?

But the tables were all low and round, and there were stools, not chairs, so people could not sit back, but rather leaned in, elbows on tabletops, better for conversation. The walls were covered with framed travel posters of the English countryside that Sam continued to collect over the years, each with its own little light. A narrow shelf ran down the whole side of the place, dropped down from the high ceiling, and there was Sam's collection of oversized chess pieces, some over three feet tall. Sam had hunted for those, too. I'd found a wooden knight in a flea market a few years ago, dark burnished wood, about twenty inches high, and Sam had been delighted.

"The chessmen?" I asked Craig.

"My mom had over a hundred," he said. He grabbed Larissa's hand and walked out, Amanda following.

I ran my hand over a worn, scarred tabletop. He'd been very particular, I remembered. And in the twenty-two years of Sam's on Main, he refused to make one change to the bar other than adding to what was already there. The dining room got a refresh every few years, but...

I hadn't known him at all, I realized. I thought I'd been the only woman he ever really loved, but there had been a woman in Brooklyn who he'd loved and never forgotten, even before he knew she'd borne him a son.

I yelled goodbye to Glory, closing the door quietly behind me.

We stopped in at Tidal Gifts. I knew that if I didn't let Stella have a good look, I'd never hear the end of it. Besides, her store was like a little treasure chest, and I knew the kids would love it.

She came scurrying in from the back as we entered, stopped, stared, then came at Craig in a rush, grabbing his hand.

"Oh, my dear boy, we are all so sorry about your dad. He was such a special man." She dropped his hand and crouched down in front of the twins. "Look at you two! Thank goodness for that freckle, or I bet even your daddy wouldn't be able to tell you apart!"

Maddie giggled. "You noticed?"

"Why, how could I not?" Stella said, beaming. "Look at it, right there, like a little drop of sunshine all curled up and napping." She stood and looked at Amanda. "And you, darling, so glad to meet you. You'll be going into middle school? My grandson is there. Can I tell him to find you at lunch? I know how awful it is to eat alone."

Amanda's jaw dropped, and she turned beet red.

Stella put her hands to her cheeks. "Oh, there I go. Butting in. I'm sorry honey, but I know what it's like to be the new girl. Just trying to help."

"No," Amanda stammered. "That's okay. Sure. Thank you."

Craig was looking around, and the twins had already made it to the back of the store where the dolls and stuffed animals were.

She looked over at me and arched her eyebrows. "Where you all off to?" she asked. "Post office?"

Craig frowned. "Why would I need to go to the post office?"

"You need a box," I explained. "There's no delivery for East-ville. You have to get your mail at the post office. And you'll need a box number to register the girls, so I guess we should go there first."

"There's no mail delivery?" Amanda asked. "Seriously?"

"Honey, it's all part of the charm of country life. We get delivery in town, but for all you out there in the boondocks..." Stella grinned. She was so good with kids. I wished I had her talent for making everyone and anyone like her. "But then, we don't get to keep goats."

Maddie came running up with a small stuffed hedgehog. "Please, Daddy? Please? We both like this one so we'll share. Please?"

Craig made an elaborate showing, sighing, dropping his head, and slumping his shoulders.

"Please?" Larissa echoed. They stood before him, two pouting, pleading adorable tots. If I was their parent, they'd be the most spoiled twins on the planet.

"Okay," Craig said at last. "I guess."

The girls jumped up and down, yelling *thank you* as Craig reached for his wallet.

Stella held up a hand. "On the house, girls. As a welcome to Cape Edwards present."

Craig started to protest, but she waved him away and stepped closer to Amanda. "Do you see something you'd like, honey?"

Amanda's eyes went around the shop quickly and came to rest on a dream catcher, hanging by the register.

"Perfect," Stella said, taking it down carefully. "Let me wrap this in something."

"You don't have to do this," Craig said.

"I know I don't," Stella agreed, smiling. "I want to."

He didn't argue, and her gifts were handed over in a bright blue bag. More thanks were said, and as we walked out, Stella called my name.

"Head to the car," I told them, and went back into the store.

"Well?" she asked.

"Well what?"

"I don't know. Is he nice? Funny? He sure looks like Sam, but... those twins are sweet, but that older girl, oh, my gosh."

"He's nice. Kind of boring. I don't think he smiles. He doesn't have Sam's...charm. He told me he wants to get a job, sell the bar, and find his own place, so this is all temporary, thank God. And yes, I could eat those little girls right up with a spoon. But Amanda..."

Stella nodded. "Keep an eye on her, Jenna. She's broken."

"I know."

She gave me a quick hug. "Thanks for bringing them in. Now, off to the post office. Terri is going to be in her glory."

I laughed. "Yes, she is. And thanks, Stella. For being so kind."

She shrugged. "Sam's family, Jenna. They're Sam's family."

Yes, they were, and as I walked back outside, I felt a little tug of envy because I wasn't Sam's family any more.

Chapter Four

Fridays had their own special routine.

I drove across the bridge—again—but this time turned south to visit my mother and sister who shared a condo right on the water. It was a tiny place, not really designed for full-time living, but rather for vacationers who only needed space for a week or two worth of belongings. So their apartment was stuffed to the gills with books and papers, knick-knacks and photo albums, and two spoiled cats. My sister was ten years older than I, and when her husband died four years ago, she talked Mom into selling her house, she sold her own place, and they bought the condo on the beach together. It was high on the fifth floor, with a balcony overlooking the ocean. The water there was the Atlantic, and it was a different from the Chesapeake as I was from my sister Sharon.

Sharon still worked. She was hostess in the dining room of one of the bigger hotels. She worked late every night, which suited her fine, because then she could spend her days sitting on the beach. She was there in all weather, under a beach umbrella in the rain or shine, sometimes wrapped in scarves and shawls against the cold. Mom preferred the balcony. They both wanted to live on the ocean and were happy as clams. I visited them every week, not out of obligation, but because they were two of my most favorite people in the world.

We had lunch on the balcony.

"So, tell us about this Craig person," Mom asked when we finally sat down to eat. They'd gotten the story the previous week, as well as the whole of my anger and frustration.

"He looks just like Sam, but they're different. Craig is very nice, but a little bland. He's a strict father."

"With twin girls, he'd have to be," Sharon said. Her three kids, all boys, were scattered up and down the Virginia coast. She was short and curvy, taking after my mother, who had morphed into a bit of a dumpling in her old age. Sharon was a looker for fifty, and I knew she had plenty of men circling her. But her husband had been a hard, bitter man, and she had blossomed since his death with a newfound freedom. I knew she had plenty of interest in attention, but no use for anything permanent in her life.

"What," my mother asked, her fork taking apart her chicken salad as though looking for bits of coal, "is an IT guy?"

"Computer stuff," I told her. "Programming and developing, I think."

"Not much of a call for that on the peninsula," Sharon said. "He's better off looking over here."

"I know. I told him that. I imagine he'll start looking during the summer."

"Funny Sam never talked about him," Mom said, finally finding a piece of chicken worthy of a bite.

"Craig said Sam never talked about me either. Or about Cape Edwards at all."

"Everyone has secrets," Sharon observed. She looked up at me through her lashes. She knew most of mine, even the things my friends never imagined.

I took a long drink of sweet tea. "Yes, I guess so. I'm just really hurt. I thought Sam trusted me."

"Trust has nothing to do with secrets, Jenna," Mom said calmly.

"That's why they're secrets." She knew about those. My father left us all when I was just six, and if Mom knew why, she never said.

My sister made terrific chicken salad, but today I was not at all hungry.

"How are the goats?" Sharon asked, changing the subject.

"They're goaty," I said. "Eating and capering around. That's pretty much all they're good for. That and the tax break I get for being a farm with livestock, instead of just a big house on the water. And the milk. At least they keep me in homemade cheese."

"That cheese you bought over to us a few weeks ago?" Mom asked. "Why, I didn't know that was from your friend Dave. That was quite lovely."

We talked then of simple things, my job, the garden, the people in town they both knew. Mom went in for her nap, and Sharon and I walked on the beach, talking some more, then not talking at all. We finally sat, close to the shore. The sun was hot and the wind was quiet. We watched the water in silence. One of the worst things about my job was the constant barrage to the senses: the noise, the stress, the level of concentration that was needed for a long twelve-hour shift. Which was why I valued time alone. And silence. Sitting here not talking with my sister was the happiest I'd been in a week.

She put her arm around my shoulder and scooted closer. "Did you really want the bar for yourself?"

I shrugged. "Yes. Maybe. The fantasy sure was tempting. I think the reality would have been a very different story. I really wanted the house for myself."

"You'll get it."

"Eventually."

"And in the meantime, I bet it's nice having company."

"Three kids and a man who has no sense of humor is not what I'd call company."

"Don't be so hard on Craig. He's had it tough, and he doesn't know you. He might be terrific."

"And what if he is?"

She sighed and tightened her grip. "Don't go too much longer alone, Jenna."

"Yeah, I know. I worry about that, sometimes."

"Worry about what?"

"Being found dead in my pajamas, surrounded by animals and empty bottles of wine."

"Jenna!"

I laughed. "Kidding! I don't like wine that much. Maybe just one bottle."

She shook her head. "Forty isn't that old."

"Neither is fifty."

"I know, and I can guarantee that I'm getting a lot more action than you are. In fact, I have a date tonight. The fourth date with the same gentleman. He's very nice."

I looked sideways at her. "The fourth date? With the same guy? Woo-woo."

"And that's pretty much how I feel with my panties down around my ankles and his mouth where it should be."

I almost choked with laughter. "Oh, big sis, you certainly are getting more action than I am."

She kissed the side of my head. "Honey, I know what Sam meant to you. But he was out of your life years ago, and you never moved on. It's time."

"Maybe. But with his son? That's just...creepy."

"I'm not talking about Craig Ferris. Obviously, besides a bit of physical attraction, I bet he's probably not your type. But Jenna, there's Match.com, Plenty O Fish...go online. Find somebody. Before you get too stuck in your ways."

"Stella said I was becoming a curmudgeon."

"Stella is a smart woman."

"Yes. She is."

We sat for a bit longer, then went back to the condo. Mom was still asleep, so I drove back to Cape Edwards.

The day wasn't over yet.

I could smell paint when I walked into the house. I also heard music. Another Disney soundtrack, I guessed. I followed the music and the laughter.

Craig and the twins were painting the big bedroom a pale, quiet pink. Drop cloths covered the furniture and carpet, and each girl had a half-sized roller and was diligently working on a small corner of the room.

"Hey, guys, this looks great."

Craig looked over. "Yes. I managed to talk them away from the Pepto-Bismol shades."

Maddie looked over her shoulder and rolled her eyes. "It's not what *I* would have picked."

"Well, maybe not, but what a difference. You know, Craig, I'm pretty sure there's hardwood under this carpet if you want to tear it up."

He set down his roller. "I was hoping you'd say that, especially since the girls found a very cool shaggy rug in the shape of a very big heart."

"Sure. Feel free to do whatever you want. After all, this is your house too. Where's Amanda?"

Craig jerked his head to the next room. "She wanted to do it herself."

I walked farther down the hall. Sure enough, Amanda was standing, roller in hand, putting a soft and quite lovely shade of green on the wall.

"Green is a relaxing color," I said. "This is going to look really nice when you're done."

She was dressed in baggy pull-on shorts and an equally baggy T-shirt. "I want to pull up the rug. Dad said we can try. The furniture's okay, but I want to paint it white. And I'd like some hanging plants. Ferns, maybe? Like the ones hanging in that sunroom?"

I nodded. "Sure. Actually, we can divide them up next week if you like. I've got tons of clay pots in the garage, or you can find really pretty ones at Del's. That's the garden center up in Cheriton." Watching her, I suddenly realized I hadn't seen her with a cell phone. She was what, twelve? Thirteen? Why wasn't she glued to the screen like other girls her age?

"You don't have a phone?" I asked.

She froze. I'd said the wrong thing. Somehow, I'd made a mistake here.

"Never mind," I said hurriedly. "We'll look at those ferns this weekend, see which ones we can cut apart."

I backed out and hurried back to the living room.

I put up the battered baby gate I'd used years ago when Finn was just a puppy and needed to be confined. I set it in the hallway going down to the bedrooms and let the dogs out of the laundry room. They ran outside first, barking and sniffing, and I walked to the edge of the water.

There was a freighter out in the bay. I saw them frequently, along with the fishing boats that passed several times a day. My favorites were the sailboats. One day, I told myself for the hundredth time, I was going to learn to sail and set off right from my own little dock.

Finn came bounding up, the legs of an unfortunate tree frog sticking out of his mouth.

"A present?" I asked.

He sat, his curly tail wagging happily.

"You know I don't like tree frogs," I told him. "Can't you kill something less gross? A mouse, maybe?" He bounded off without answering.

Maybe Sharon was right. I needed to get a little bit more of a life if I was spending my time talking more to my dogs than to people.

I went back into the house, took a shower, and got ready for Friday night.

Cape Edwards was a town of many faces. It was a beach town, a vacation spot during the summer, and a fishing village all year round. It also had a surprising arty side. There were six art galleries on Main Street, and three bars had music all summer, the entertainment picked from our very talented local pool. There was also a playhouse that managed at least six productions a year, a small bookstore with readings once a month by local authors, and at least six different book clubs. The Grove Gallery on Main Street had a live event every Friday night. A musician, a lecture, a reading...anything to get a small crowd gathered. They also served free wine and cheese, so going to the Grove had become, for many of us, a sort of cocktail hour before dinner and moving on to the rest of the evenings entertainment. I was never alone. Terri was with me, or Karen, and Stella or Marie, if they were around. We always stopped at the Grove, then had dinner at Shorty's or Sam's on Main, or we'd walk all the way over to Treacher's, right on the marina. Then we'd go off to whatever venue had the singer or group we fancied. Sometimes, we even hopped into Terri's golf cart and headed out to BayHarbor, a planned community right at the edge of town with condos, townhouses, a small marina and a long pier with a crab shack and stage at the very end.

I explained this all, very briefly, to Craig, who just nodded. "Girls night? Okay. Have fun."

I got to the Grove just as Sandy poured the first glass of wine. I wasn't a big wine drinker, but I always took a glass to be polite.

She leaned across the counter. "I saw you all yesterday, and Sam's son came in here this afternoon with his little girls. They'd been at the beach, he told me. Very nice."

I snagged a slice of smoked Gouda and a cracker. "Yep."

"Is he staying?"

"Nope." And I moved away.

Terri found me the minute she walked in. "I can't believe Craig looks so much like Sam. Is it freaking you out?"

I nodded. "A little bit." She'd been on her best behavior when I'd taken Craig in the day before, helping him fill out the form for his PO box and explaining all the little idiosyncrasies of the rural postal service. She'd given the girls lollipops and hadn't peppered any of them with questions. But I knew they were coming.

"What's the plan? Do you know?"

"He's going to look for a job, probably across the Bay, sell the bar and move on. Tell anyone interested they have to move fast." I raised my eyebrows. "You interested?"

"Oh, honey," she fanned herself with her open hand as she leaned closer. "Steve McCann came in today, and can I tell you? We had quite a moment."

I frowned. "Is he the beard?" Both brothers were pretty good looking, fiftyish, and all that hard construction work had left them with bodies a college athlete would envy. One was taller with very dark hair. The other had hair turning gray and a neatly trimmed beard he'd been wearing even before the hipsters decided beards were cool.

"No. The beard is Mike. Steve is the taller one. I asked him, hell, practically invited him here tonight, but he said he'd be working out in Quinby."

Karen came up holding two glasses of wine. She handed one to Terri. "If you were over here without a drink, I figured it was pretty hot stuff. What's going on?"

"Terri and Steve McCann had a moment."

Karen's eyes popped. "Oh?"

Terri nodded and gulped half her wine. "He's working out in Quinby. Is there anything to work on in Quinby?"

"Sure," Karen said. "Maybe."

"Too bad your condo is so perfect," I said to Terri. "Otherwise you could hire him for some work." Terri lived right on Main Street. She'd bought a newly renovated condo just five years ago, located, luckily enough for her, right over a very nice shop that sold wine and cheese. Her place was gorgeous, and had a spacious balcony overlooking Main Street and the marina.

She chewed her lip, a sure sign of serious thinking. "You're right. I need to get him to work for me." Her eyes suddenly opened wide. "Hey, remember my old college roommate? Chris Polittano? She's been down a bunch of times."

I nodded, vividly remembering a tiny, very pretty woman who drank like a fish and dared us all to go skinny-dipping in the bay one night. "Yes, I remember her. Why?"

"Well, she'd been taking care of her mom, who just died, and she left her boyfriend, over a year ago now, and she was saying she needed a change, and I told her she should move down here. And she liked the idea." She grabbed my arm and shook it. "That place, right on Main down from Bogey's? That dilapidated cottage? She could buy that. And I could help her do the renovation and remodeling."

Karen gave her the side-eye. "You don't know anything about renovating *or* remodeling, Terri. Jenna here had to help you hang your pictures, for God's sake."

"I know! That's the best part. I'd have to hire the McCann brothers! Oh, this is the best idea I've ever had." She looked at her empty glass and hurried over to Sandy.

Karen looked at me, eyebrows raised. "Is she going to buy a house just to meet a man?" she asked.

I shook my head. "No, I don't think so. I think *Chris* is going to buy the house."

"Oh." Karen shrugged. "Okay then."

Judd Mitchell, handsome, bald-headed, with a very expensive camera permanently around his neck, sidled up. "Don't suppose he's gay?" he whispered.

I shook my head. "Sorry."

He sighed. "All of the good ones are straight," he muttered.

Karen and I burst out laughing.

"How are you, Judd?" He was in his forties and had come down from Baltimore ten years ago to photograph the demolition of the old concrete plant and never left.

He shrugged. "Lonely."

Karen looked up at him. "Hey, I'm lonely too, you know."

He bent down and kissed her cheek. "Tell you what. In ten years, if we're both still single, we'll get a place together and spend all day watching old sitcoms and eating chips and onion dip."

Karen poked him with her elbow. "If I'm still single in ten years I'll blow my brains out." She sniffed. "But the chip and dip part sounds pretty good."

He wandered off. I looked around the Grove.

This was my life. These familiar people, these same places. I was comfortable and safe, occasionally happy and generally content. Tonight I would hear two people I'd never heard of perform music that I'd probably enjoy, and then never see or hear them again. Then I'd have a good dinner with good friends, listen to a small jazz band out on the pier, then go home and sleep. Alone. Tomorrow I'd work in the garden and walk my dogs, but tomorrow there would be three little girls, painting rooms I never used, going in and out of my kitchen and living room. Would they chase the dogs? Get in my garden?

I shook my head. The children that Sam and I had wanted, filling rooms and chasing dogs, were not mine. They belonged to a cautious, quiet man who would leave my house and take those girls with him.

I had to be careful to remember that.

We'd talked a lot the night before, but as always, Saturday break-fast was a time for serious conversation about serious things.

"Terri," Stella began, "please tell me you're not going to buy a house just to have an excuse to talk to Steve McCann."

Wendy had taken our order and we were all stirring coffee.

"No."

Karen looked over the top of her reading glasses at Stella. "See? I told you she was just drunk when she said it."

"Actually, I wasn't drunk," Terri said. "And what I did say was that I was going to get *Chris* to buy a house. Isn't that what I said, Jenna?"

I nodded. "Yes, it is. The Farnham place, way down on Main. You also said it was the best idea you ever had, which I think might be up for debate."

Stella patted Terri's hand. "Listen, I know you've been watching that man ever since you and Dave broke up, but don't you think this is a bit extreme?"

I looked at Terri, surprised. "Really that long? Why didn't I know this?"

She shrugged. "Jenna, you spend a lot of time in your own head. You miss all sorts of stuff."

"Well, okay, maybe, but Dave left almost a year ago. Steve McCann? Am I really the only one who didn't know this?"

Karen sighed noisily. "It hasn't been widely discussed, if that's what you mean. But every time his name is mentioned her eyes get all round and soft, and her lower lip trembles."

Stella and Marie laughed, and Terri swatted Karen's hand. "My lip don't tremble for *no* man."

Marie shook her head. "Actually, the Farnham house is a good investment. Zoned commercial, you know. It was a pretty decent beach rental for years. I'll never know why old Mr. Farnham's kid just let it go like that. If he'd sold it right after he died, it would have been worth quite a bit more."

"So now," Terri said, folding her hands, "It's dirt cheap. I looked on Zillow this morning and sent Chris the link. It looked pretty bad in the photos, but it wouldn't take much to make it *so* cute. And then Chris could live right here in Cape Edwards. I know she'd fit right in."

"Doesn't Chris have, like, a job?" I asked. I hated to be the party pooper, but...

"Well, yes. She's got her own real estate office on Rehoboth."

I almost spit out my coffee. "She's where? Rehoboth *Delaware?* You expect her to give up her own office and move down here where there are six established realtors fighting over the same ten houses?"

Wendy came by, laden with food. "And you know that my mother gets anything and everything that's worth selling. Those other offices are starving on the dregs. I forgot toast." She went back to the kitchen.

Terri sighed and poured syrup on her pancakes "Chris really doesn't a job. She got a bunch of money when her mom died." She froze, and her eyes lit up. "She could be a flipper! You know, buying crappy houses, fixing them up, and then she could sell them. I could be her partner." The woman's eyes were practically popping out of her head. "We could have our own TV show!"

"Oh dear," Stella muttered.

"What?" Terri asked, indignant. "I bet we'd be great on TV."

Wendy returned with toast. "Mom said they dropped the price on the Farnham place again. Want her to give you a call, Terri?"

Terri nodded, her mouth full of pancake.

"Oh dear," Stella said again. She turned to me. "Craig seems very nice. A bit...somber."

I shook my head. "Somber is right. I have not seen him smile once. Totally devoid of a sense of humor."

"Now, Jenna," Karen chided. "Is that really fair? He was going through a divorce, then his wife died, then his father died, and he had to move out of his house. What, exactly, were you expecting?"

God, I hated it when she was reasonable. "I don't know," I grumbled. "Something else."

Stella was spreading grape jam on her toast. "You wanted him to be like Sam," she said. "Because he *looked* so much like Sam. But let's face it, that man was one of a kind. And genetics can only go so far." She pointed her knife at me as she spoke. "You be careful not to get Sam and his son confused in your brain. They are obviously two very different people, and you would do well to keep reminding yourself of that." She took a bite of toast and chewed, then swallowed. "In other news, that new doctor came into the shop last night. Very nice looking. Alone. I tried to shoo her down to the Grove, but she said she was just, how did she put it? Easing into the neighborhood." She grinned. "She's a sister. Dreadlocks halfway down her back. I'd say midforties? It was very nice to see another successful black woman right here in Cape Edwards. Dara French is her name. She bought towels, two sets of coasters and a martini pitcher."

"Well, that's certainly helpful," Terri said. "Obviously, she's an antisocial alcoholic."

Marie sniffed. "Maybe not. Could be she's stockpiling for a

great big open house once all her renovations are done. Now, there's an idea, Terri. You could go over there and volunteer to put up sheetrock. That way, you'll get close to Steve and give us the scoop on Dr. French."

Subtle sarcasm was sometimes lost on Terri. She looked offended. "First of all, I know nothing about sheetrock. Second, Steve might not even be there. He might be up in Quinby, and I'm certainly not going to drive all the way up *there*." She looked around. "And I already met Dr. French. She came into the post office and was lovely."

"She's a fine looking woman. I may have to get my sexy back on." Stella said smugly.

"Do we know her specialty?" Karen asked. "I could develop symptoms."

Stella reached over and slapped Karen's hand. "You like men, and I know it, so don't even *try* to get me riled."

Karen grinned. "You know I am an equal opportunity lover."

We all laughed, and the conversation drifted away from men to the turn in the weather, then the upcoming season. But in the back of my mind was Craig Ferris. What would it take to get that man to smile?

And why did I even care?

Chapter Five

✥

When I got home, the Suburban was gone. I changed into my gardening clothes—overalls, T-shirt and my old Doc Martens. I went into the kitchen to get a bottle of water, and when I opened my refrigerator, I froze.

It was full of food.

Usually, I had on hand a few basics. Diet Coke. Beer. A rotisserie chicken. Mayonnaise. Cream for my coffee, bread and butter, eggs and cheese. A few containers of takeout and five different mustards.

But this...this was *food*. There were actually green things in the vegetable bins instead of stray water bottles, and there was orange juice and apple juice, yogurt and six-packs of chocolate pudding.

I opened the freezer. Frozen waffles, frozen burritos, ice cream and ground meat. I pulled out a package and looked at it. Yes, ground meat, and chicken breasts, pork chops...

I sure hoped someone knew how to cook.

I opened the cabinet and noticed boxes of cookies and crackers, three kinds of cereal, boxed macaroni and cheese. Another cabinet held cans of Spaghetti-O's, cans of soup, cans of tuna fish... how much could three little girls eat?

I wandered down the hallway, following the faint smell of paint. The twins' room looked considerably better: light and bright, the furniture rearranged to create two very separate spaces. Amanda's room already had a few posters on the walls. It, too, looked much better. I took a peek into the last bedroom. No painting here. The bed was in the same spot, neatly made. No pile of clothes in the corner, no shoes lying by the closet door.

This was no longer *my* house. The house I had lived in for so long would never have had pink walls and fresh vegetables in the refrigerator. Sam's family were slowly creeping in, making their own spaces, and even though nothing was being taken away from me exactly, I still felt like I was losing a bit of something that had been only mine.

I went back through the house, out the front door, and into the garden.

My garden, I must say, was a thing of beauty. It was completely fenced in, had six raised beds, and a long worktable at one end. I'd managed to keep most critters out. I had to build the fence high enough that I could cover the whole thing with chicken wire to keep the birds from swooping down and eating everything.

It was still evolving. This year I put in asparagus beds for the first time in a corner spot where the kale used to be. I knew I wouldn't get anything this year, but it was always the first place I looked.

I spent two hours weeding and checking my seeds. Nothing had sprouted, but it was still early. The tomato plants were the ones I'd bought the week before at Del's, and I planted them and set up their cages. Then I watered and turned my compost pile. This, at least, was still all mine. When I was done, I was sweaty and filthy. I never wore gloves unless I was doing heavy lifting, and I forgot to put the soap under my fingernails, so my hands looked pretty rough.

I went into the house, washed up quickly and made a pitcher of iced tea. While I was waiting for the bags to steep, I went back out and walked to the Bay.

Sam had always talked about a deck or patio, but I liked the grass. My favorite Adirondack chair was close to the water, a rickety table next to it, just big enough for a mug of coffee. I sat and watched the sun on the water, thinking about the rest of my day. I had to clean out the goat pen, maybe take a few of them out for a walk. Yeah, I know—walking goats? But I couldn't trust them, out and running free to not wander off, or wade into the Bay, or go diving off the dock. On the occasions they did get out, Dave would round them up and bring them back, but trying to catch a runaway goat was not an easy task, unless the goat was very hungry and you were holding a favorite treat.

And then what? Some Saturday nights were potluck nights. I'd invite my friends over, and they would each bring a dish. They'd all tasted my cooking before and knew that I could be trusted only with apple pie for dessert. But tonight I'd be on my own except for Craig and his daughters. What were we going to do? Obviously, finding an old MGM musical and singing along might not fly with my company. But they *weren't* my company, I didn't have to entertain them, and I wasn't about to change my life to accommodate them. They were the interlopers here, no matter what Sam's will said. Why should I be the one to tiptoe around?

Finn came racing out into the yard, yapping like a mad thing. I looked to see what'd gotten him so excited and saw Larissa — or was it Maddie? — chasing him. I couldn't see the freckle from here, but whoever she was, she and Finn were having a great time. Chloe trotted out next, and Bit sped by, stopped to pee, then scrambled up on my lap.

It was Larissa who grabbed Finn and wrestled him to the ground in front of me.

"Whatcha' doin'?"

"Watching the water."

She looked out dutifully. "What's it doing?"

I laughed. "Just being water, I guess. Did you guys go shopping?"

She nodded. "Yes. We bought a whole bunch of stuff. Daddy sent me to keep the dogs busy while he unloaded the car."

I felt a pang. Should I offer to help? Did they even *need* my help? After all, there were more of them. And they were all perfectly capable of hollering if they needed anything from me. Unless Amanda...

I got up and went inside. "Craig?" I called. The front door was open, and I saw Amanda come in, holding a huge bag from Home-Goods. I ran up and took it from her.

"New bedspread?" I asked.

She nodded gratefully. "Yes. Thanks. It wasn't that heavy in the store."

"It never is," I told her, and followed her into her room. "More?"

She nodded again, and I went out front.

How he managed to get a whole dresser *in* the back of the Suburban was beyond me, but Craig was having a few issues getting it back out. I came up beside him. "Need some help?"

He nodded. "If you could just grab the other side..."

It came out slowly, solid wood, white, and heavier than it looked. We eased it on to the gravel.

"How many guys did it take to put this in there?" I asked.

"Only two," Craig answered, stretching to the side and wincing. "But I think one was named Hercules."

Did he just make a joke? I choked on a laugh. "I believe you. I have a hand truck in the garage. Hold on."

As I pulled up the garage door, I felt a pang. Living alone had given me blinders to certain behaviors, and as I saw the inside of my garage in the sudden blare of sunlight, I realized I was on track for an intervention from the team at *Hoarders*. I was used to the idea that finding anything in my garage usually required a good map and a Sherpa, but having a stranger see all that mess...

As I pulled up the garage door, Craig, behind me, let out a low whistle. "Any chance it will come if you call it?"

Another joke? I stared at him.

"What?" he asked.

"I was beginning to think you had no sense of humor whatsoever."

His mouth twitched into a possible smile. "Well, Jenna, I don't really know you, do I? I was worried that if I let all my charm and intellect out at once, it would be too much for you."

I grinned. "I'll try to hold myself back. Look, there it is. See? I put red tape on the handles so it would be easier to find."

He brushed past me, or at least he tried. I was backed up against the John Deere tractor, the one that I hadn't started in years and couldn't move. We were chest to chest, and stuck.

"I can't move," I told him.

"Sure you can," he said, and he grabbed me around the waist and lifted me, straight up in the air.

In my defense, I had no way of knowing he was going to do that, so it was perfectly natural for me to yelp in surprise. And throw my arms around his neck, holding on for dear life. And clamp my knees around his hips.

He froze. We were nose to nose, and I could see tiny green flecks in his brown eyes. His breath was warm against my chin. He turned slowly, a quarter turn, and set me down. My knees loosened and my feet hit the floor, and I backed away so fast I almost fell over.

"See? You can move," he said. He turned back into the garage and pushed his way to the hand truck, picked it up, held it over his head, and came back out.

I stood, feeling the blood rush to my face, watching him go back toward the Suburban. I felt like I had never in my life been more aware of a man's body as I had been of his in those few seconds. I'd felt the hard bone of his shoulders, the shifting of muscle as he'd held me. My reaction, purely physical, left me shaken.

I was also aware that I was covered in dried sweat and compost, my hair had half-slipped out of its topknot, and there was probably at least one smudge of dirt on my face. Why hadn't I showered? And changed? Changed into something soft and flattering and preferably slightly see through?

That pulled me up short. Where did *that* come from?

He looked over his shoulder, totally unfazed, and jerked his head for me to follow him.

We got the hand truck, maneuvered the dresser on, and wheeled it into the house. It was narrow and tall, and fit perfectly in the corner.

Maddie and Larissa were already getting their new bedspreads on their beds. Maddie had a simple quilt in pink, purple and green. Larissa had gone with a Moana theme, blue ocean and a fierce looking little girl.

"Looking good, guys," I told them.

Maddie was looking at me rather critically. "Were you working in a mine today?" she asked.

"Maddie." Craig said sternly.

I waved it off. "Perfectly legitimate question. Actually, I was in the garden all morning, and I didn't shower because next I have to clean up where the goats are. They make a whole lotta poop."

Larissa stood before me, bouncing. "Can I help you? Please? I really wanted to play with those goats yesterday, but Daddy said I had to ask you first. Are they friendly? Do they bite? Is that gray spotted one a boy or girl? 'Cause I think her name is probably Esmeralda or Anastasia or maybe Jasmine."

Actually, his name was Jack. "They don't bite, but sometimes if you feed them and your fingers are in the way, you can feel a nibble."

Maddie joined her. "Really? Oh, I want to get nibbled. Can I get nibbled? What do they eat, anyway?"

"They eat everything," I told them. "They're goats. You can help me walk them. They like to get out once in a while and check out the woods." I looked at Craig. "Are they released from bedroom duty?"

He nodded, and his mouth twitched again. "Sure. I'll hang with Amanda."

The girls disappeared in a flash. Craig and I stood, looking at each other. He was dressed in dark wash jeans and a polo shirt with a familiar logo on the pocket, bare ankles above leather docksides. I looked less polished. "I see you went grocery shopping. Did you empty out the Food Lion?"

He did it. He smiled. Sam's smile, warm and sweet. "The woman who checked me out, Ruth? She told me to tell you Sara Lee is on special tomorrow. She was a very friendly woman."

I smiled back. "Yes, she is. She's been checking me out since I was sixteen years old. She knows all my food secrets."

"Food secrets? Is that even a thing?"

"Oh, sure. Sara Lee cheesecake, puffed Cheetos, Dr. Browns Root Beer...I got a hundred of 'em."

"Ah. Well, I'm making meatloaf and mac and cheese tonight. Are you going to be around, or will you be out again?"

I cleared my throat. "I'll be around."

"Good. We'll be eating around six."

"Thanks. I'll be sure to shower."

"What? And wash away all that sexy earth mother thing you've got going on right now?"

My jaw dropped, and I let out a whoop. Apparently, he had a sense of humor after all.

Wait.

Did he say sexy?

Maddie, Larissa, and I walked the goats. The girls each had one each on a leash, and I had four. The girls had argued for a more equal distribution, insisting they could each walk two at the same time as well, but I knew better. The critters may have been small, but they were strong, and if they headed in opposite directions at the same time, it would get dicey. I was used to them. Chloe and Finn came with us, and we walked down the drive and almost over to Dave Robinson's place. Dave was out by his beehives, and when I explained that Dave was helping the bees make honey, the thrill of the goats were completely forgotten and the twins wanted to run right over and take a look. I had to explain that the bees weren't necessarily tame, and if we did go over, we'd surely get stung.

So, back to walking goats. And they talked.

They talked about Sam coming to visit them. About how Mommy and Daddy lived in different places until Mommy died, then Daddy moved in with them. They talked about their other grandpa, and their grandma, and how Grandpa and his new wife wanted the twins to live with them. They had quite an argument about Amanda, and how many times she ran away right after Mommy and Daddy split up. They also talked about how Amanda was bullied by some bad girls at school until Daddy took her phone away so she wouldn't have to see.

I stopped wondering why he didn't smile much.

When we got back, they helped me shovel goat poop, set out clean straw, rinsed out the feed buckets, and Maddie tried to comb Jasmine's long coat. Jack stood still for about two minutes before kicking out his hind legs and running off to another corner. We finally came dragging into the house after four o'clock.

Craig was sitting in the living room, reading. He'd taken the Hamilton biography off of my bookshelf. He looked up as we came in and held up the book.

"I hope you don't mind," he said. "It's been on my TBR pile for a while."

He had a TBR pile.

I shook my head. "No, feel free. But these two might need to be hosed off." He stood, then bent down and sniffed Maddie's hair. "Is that what goat smells like?" he asked.

Maddie and Larissa started to giggle.

"Must be," Craig went on in a very serious voice, "because I have never smelt *anything* like that in Chicago."

The giggles got louder.

"Not, even," he went on, "in the *zoo*."

Full out laughter now, and he stooped to pick them up, one under each arm, and they all headed off to the bathroom.

I went into the kitchen. My sweet tea was done. I took out the tea bags and put the pitcher in the refrigerator between the apple juice and the container of cut-up cantaloupe, two items that had never been in my refrigerator before. Then I went off to my own shower, stopping in the laundry room. I kicked off my Doc Martens and peeled off my socks, dropping them directly into the washer. Next came my overalls and T-shirt. I then went back into the hall and headed toward the linen closet for a towel.

"Ah..."

I froze, sighed, crossed my arms over my bare boobs, and turned around.

Craig looked embarrassed, but I had to admire him for keeping his eyes on my face. "I'm really sorry."

I shrugged and hugged myself a little tighter. "My fault. I'll have to remember I don't live alone anymore, and wandering around the house in my underwear has to stop."

His mouth twitched again. "I just...I need more towels."

I was trapped. My bedroom door was about three feet behind Craig. I had nowhere to go but into the linen closet, which wasn't going to work very well.

"Sure," I backed up and jerked my head to the left. "Linen closet right here. Take what you need."

He hurried forward and opened the closet door. I backed into the corner, standing behind the now open closet door. "How are you for blankets?" I asked. I leaned forward just a bit and could see his back as he went through a few towels, looking for the right size.

He nodded, his entire head *in* the linen closet, as he pulled out three or four towels. "Good. We'll do a load or two tomorrow, if that's okay."

I cleared my throat, trying to ignore the fact that we were having a conversation with me practically naked, huddled in a corner, my panties, literally, working themselves into a twist. "Why don't I take Monday as my official laundry day? I only need a load or two a week. You've got a lot more to do, so any other day is yours."

He closed the linen closet and immediately put his back to me. "That sounds like a good idea."

"Okay then."

He went back down the hall. I closed my eyes and breathed out slowly.

Well, at least my panties didn't have any holes in them.

Craig certainly knew his way around a kitchen. He must have done a little snooping around mine, because he knew exactly where things were, including my ceramic loaf pan which I hadn't seen since the last time I'd made banana bread, two Christmases ago.

Amanda was chopping things when I emerged, freshly washed and decently dressed, not smelling of goat and with all the garden soil scraped out from under my fingernails. She looked up as I walked in and gave me a small smile, then bent her head to her task. She was dicing celery, and each piece seemed to be the exact same size.

"Need help?" I asked.

Craig shook his head. "No, we've got this covered." No sly, lustful glances. No suggestive raised eyebrows or naughty smirk. He seemed as eager to put what happened twenty minutes ago out of his mind as I was.

I opened the fridge. "Mind if I grab a beer?"

He shook his head, intent on his cooking.

I watched him for a few minutes. "We need some music. Amanda, is there anyone you want to listen to? I've got Amazon Music, Pandora, you name it."

She brightened. "Amazon? Kelly Clarkson, please."

I grinned at her. "That's the ticket. Some girl power." I went into the living room, connected my iPhone, then the Bluetooth, and went back to the kitchen.

Both Craig and Amanda were humming. It was a big hit for Kelly, so even I knew the words. Amanda started singing along, her voice thin but sweet. Then Craig joined in, a deep, surprising baritone. They sang to each other, with each other, until they were a performance, complete with dramatic gestures, elaborate eye rolls, and a hip shaking dance-along. I watched them, and felt an ache to join them. When they were done, I burst into applause.

Amanda immediately ducked her head and turned deep red. Craig, on the other hand, took a deep bow. "Here till Thursday, folks," he intoned.

Amanda giggled.

On cue, Maddie and Larissa came tearing in, saw me, and each grabbed a hand.

"Come see our room."

"We put all the clothes in the new dresser."

"And we have pillows."

"And the stuffed animals are out."

I followed them in, was pushed onto the bed, and they began to show me. Everything. After the first five minutes, Craig came in and handed me my beer.

He leaned over and whispered. "If you just get up and leave, it will probably take them ten minutes to notice."

But I stayed with them. They were fascinating to watch, those two almost identical little people. When they were explaining to me, they spoke slowly and carefully, but to each other, it was as though they had their own language, a combination of verbal shorthand and lightning fast gestures. I finally did stand up and walk out without causing a ripple in their conversation.

Craig was making macaroni and cheese from scratch. I knew this, not because I'd ever done it myself, but because I could find no other explanation as to why he would be grating a block of cheddar cheese into a steaming pot of white sauce. There were also green beans on the stove. Not canned, but fresh, simmering with some bacon and onion.

"From scratch?" I asked. "And are those real breadcrumbs?"

He nodded. "They like the boxed stuff for lunches and snacks, but nothing beats homemade with meatloaf. Right Amanda?"

Amanda was pouring some sort of batter, chocolate, into a square pan.

"Brownies?" I asked, moving closer to look.

She nodded, her face tight. "I used your pan. I hope you don't mind."

"Mind? Are you kidding? For brownies, you could use my grandmother's china. You guys cook like this all the time?"

She carefully scraped the bowl clean, then frowned. "Like what?"

"You know..." I waved my empty beer can. Craig and Amanda looked at me as though I suggested they were in the middle of some ancient Druid ceremony. I'd forgotten that not everyone lived on takeout. "Never mind." I got another beer.

I dressed for the occasion. I'd blown out my hair, put on decent jeans and a light cotton sweater, and even smudged a bit of mascara on. After all, Craig looked like he stepped out of an ad for Polo Sport. I felt it was the least I could do.

I hopped up and sat on the counter, sipping my beer, watching him. "Did you always cook?"

He nodded. " I worked in the kitchen in my mom's place growing up. I enjoy it."

"So, you *do* know about restaurants and bars and business?"

He shook his head. "No. I know about peeling potatoes and how to tell if food has gone bad. Just because I learned to cook doesn't mean I can run a restaurant."

"It's just that Sam's on Main is more than just a restaurant. Off-season, everybody gathers there. It's...our place, more than any other place on Main Street."

"I'm sure that if Glory owned it, nothing would change."

I nodded. "You're right. But Glory would have to get a loan to buy you out. A big one, and one bad summer could close her down."

He carefully poured his mac and cheese into a Pyrex dish,

grabbed a handful of breadcrumbs in one hand, and sprinkled them over. Then, he put his dish and Amanda's brownies in the oven and set the timer. "I'm going to sell," he said.

"Okay."

"Look, Sam left me a bit of money, so you don't have to worry about buying me out right away. I know the appraisal was pretty steep."

Steep? It had been straight vertical, all the way up to the sky.

I cleared my throat. "I was thinking you could take half of the acreage outright, and I could just buy half of the house. That way, I won't have to sell my kidney to buy you out. Four acres with bay front would be easy for you to sell, or you could build your own place."

He looked thoughtful. "I'll think about that. It's not a bad idea."

Relief flooded through me. Maybe I wouldn't end up mortgaged to my eyeballs after all.

"So, he bought this house?" Craig asked. "And the bar? Where did he get all the money?"

I shook my head. "He never talked about his family. I know he was an only child, and his father was a banker, and his mother came from Boston. I assumed he just inherited it all. When we were married, there was always money for whatever we wanted." I shrugged. "I was eighteen. I didn't ask questions, you know?"

Amanda was sitting back at the table, so quietly I had almost forgotten she was there. I smiled at her. "Want to go out before dinner and look at the water?"

She jumped up, eyes bright. "Yes, please. And we bought some white paint. Is there a place I can paint my furniture?"

Craig sniffed. "Not the garage."

I shot him a look. "No, not the garage. But there's enough of an overhang by the laundry room, and there's a tiny cement spot that would be perfect."

We went back outside and walked around the house, into the garden, and out to the water. She was not like her sisters. Every word had to be coaxed out, every response carefully measured. We talked about the fern-in-her-room situation and agreed to separate two ferns as soon as she could get some pretty pots. She told me she liked to cook, too. No, she wasn't looking forward to a new school. She didn't like changes, she said.

We walked back to the house just as the meatloaf and brownies came out, a mixture of smells so comforting and homelike I almost forgot that four strangers were ruining my life.

Luckily, Methodists weren't big on formality, and I'd been going to church in jeans and a T-shirt for the past four years. That Sunday, when I walked into the kitchen, Craig was dressed in khakis and a button-down shirt. He was wearing a tie. The girls were in dresses. They looked up expectantly.

"We left you some scrambled eggs," Craig said. "And we'd like to take you up on your offer to go to church."

Offer to go to church? When had I done that?

Oh right. Last night before I ran off to my room, leaving Craig and the girls in front of the big-screen. I'd crawled into bed with the latest Harlan Coben and managed to read for almost an hour before falling asleep sitting up, the book still on my lap.

I smiled and found a plate, served myself some eggs, poured coffee and sat for breakfast.

"Is the pastor nice?"

"Do they sing? I like the singing part."

"Is there Sunday school? I hate Sunday school."

"Larissa," Craig said sternly.

Larissa slumped in her chair but looked up at me from under her eyelashes and rolled her eyes.

"The pastor is very nice, there's lots of singing, and there are two Sunday school classes. We'll go down after the service for coffee and muffins, and you can meet some people."

I glanced at Amanda, who shrank, just a little, farther back into her chair. Craig looked at his older daughter, and I saw something in his eyes, a flicker of concern.

"Do you want to stay home?" he asked her softly.

She shook her head. "No. I want to come."

I finished my eggs, excused myself from the table, and went in to change, out of my jeans and into a skirt, realized I hadn't shaved my legs in at least three weeks and changed into a much longer skirt, finally putting on a cardigan for a finishing touch.

We arrived early. The last thing I wanted was for them to arrive when the pews were already full and have the entire congregation turn to stare as they walked in. Our pastor, Carole Wilkerson, welcomed them from the pulpit, and afterward we went down into the basement and had hot coffee and homemade muffins and banana bread.

I stood to the side with Terri and watched. The twins managed to speak to every single person there. Craig was attentive and even almost smiled a couple of times. Amanda stood very close to him, not speaking, occasionally smiling shyly.

"I got him to smile," I told Terri.

"Oh, good."

"He cooks. I had the best meatloaf of my life last night."

She looked sideways at me. "Oh?"

"He said it was a mixture of beef and pork, and he sautéed the onion before mixing them in. It was so moist I didn't need ketchup. And homemade mac and cheese. *Three* cheeses, he told me. Almost as good as DeeDee's. He does his own laundry and he reads."

"Are you putting together his Tinder profile?"

"No. Just, you know, keeping you in the loop."

"Thanks. I didn't know there *was* a loop."

"Well, there is now."

"You're wearing a skirt."

"I know. Well, look at them, all dressed up like real churchgoers. I felt like I had to step it up a little."

"Yes. He cleans up well."

"He's *always* dressed nice. I don't think he ever gets dirty. Or messy."

Terri made a small noise. "You make that sound like it's a bad thing."

I shook my head, slowly, watching him. "No, it's not that. He's just so tightly wound. I wonder what he'd be like if he just loosened up a little."

"Well, it looks like Monica is trying to loosen him up right now."

She was right. Monica Waltz, new to town from Richmond, touched his arm so many times I was surprised she didn't just take a big old hand stamp and mark "He's Mine" on his forehead.

"Looks like she's trying pretty hard," I said.

"They all are. So, Chris is coming down next week to look at that house."

"Terri, are you serious? My gosh, just for Steve McCann?"

She was watching Craig. His back was toward us so we could see the faces of all the women hovering around him. "It's better than finding out what church he goes to and getting in line."

She had a point.

"Do you like him?" She asked.

"I'm not sure. Now that I've met him, I don't hate the very fact of his existence, so that's good. He's guarded. Not big on talking."

She rolled her eyes. "You really haven't spent much time with men lately, have you? Do you think he likes you?"

"I doubt it."

"What makes you say that?"

I shrugged. "Just a feeling. We should really sit down and hash this out, but like I said, he's not much of a talker."

"God, is that Olivia? I didn't know she belonged. I thought she went to the Lutheran Church, down in Capeville."

"She probably spent all morning cruising all the church parking lots, looking for an out-of-state license plate."

Terri choked back a laugh. Olivia, gushing over Craig, caught

75

my eye. I waved. She looked away, back to Craig, her red mouth smiling, showing very white teeth.

Amanda turned around, saw me, and stuck her finger down her throat, making a gagging motion. She then turned back to Olivia, her hands folded behind her back.

I felt a rush of happiness, as though Amanda and I had suddenly bonded over something very special.

"At least his daughter knows what's going on," Terri said.

"He saw me naked," I said.

Terri grabbed my arm. "What?"

"Well, I had on panties. You know how I wander around the house with no clothes on."

"Were you at least wearing a bra?"

I shot her a look. "I haven't worn a bra in years, Terri. Have you *seen* my boobs lately?"

She sighed. "I always kind of envied you for that," she said. Terri was quite shapely, and her breasts needed their own zip code. "I sag so much these days I may start looking for whalebone corsets." She nudged me. "You need to go rescue that man."

"I guess." I walked up behind Craig and tapped him on the shoulder. "Ready to head out?"

His eyes lit up, and I got another smile, this one of pure gratitude. "Oh, yes." He called the twins, who scampered over, smiling and chattering. Amanda stayed close to Craig's side and we went upstairs. I glanced back. Olivia Kopecknie was staring at me so hard I thought her eyeballs would fall out.

I waved at her again and went out the door.

Chapter Six

I explained to Craig that I left for work every morning by five thirty, and that I wouldn't be back until after eight. The dogs used the doggy door to get in and out, and they were used to waiting for their supper. I didn't know what to expect when I got home that Monday. Would the dogs remember that Craig and his daughters were friends? Or would I find them all trapped in the Suburban as I had just five days before?

When I pulled up in front of the house, they didn't even bark.

As I walked through the door, Finn raised his head and wagged his tail. Chloe got up, came over for a quick sniff, then went back to her usual spot by the fireplace. Bit didn't even get off Amanda's lap.

They were all in the living room. Craig was reading, Amanda was scratching Bit behind the ears, and Maddie and Larissa were on the floor in front of the coffee table, industriously writing in workbooks. They looked comfortable. They looked like they belonged there. I didn't know if I felt happy about that or annoyed.

"Good first day of school?" I asked.

"We're in the same classroom."

"We're probably going to have to wear name tags *forever*."

"Mrs. Keller is really nice."

"The playground here is cool."

"The boys are not very cute."

"Lunch was terrible. I hate ravioli."

"Wait." I held up a hand. "How can you hate the ravioli in the school cafeteria? That seems impossible."

"It was gross."

"And they served lettuce with pink dressing."

"But the cookie was good."

"Yes! Excellent cookie."

"Amanda?" I asked. She looked up. "How was your day?"

She shrugged. "That lady's son? The one from the store? He sat with me at lunch so that was good."

"Her grandson. Tyrell. He's a nice boy."

She shrugged again. "Yes."

I had my Wendy's takeout bag in my hand. I held it up. "I'm going to eat my dinner, guys. Later."

I went into the kitchen. It was cleaner than it had been that morning, and here was a plate on the counter. A plate containing a chicken leg and thigh, some roasted potatoes and sliced carrots.

"We saved you dinner," Craig said. "I didn't realize you'd bring your own." He picked up the plate and put in in the refrigerator. "It won't go to waste."

"Oh." I set my bag down, the smell of cheeseburger and cooling French fries filling the room. "That's...wow. That was so nice of you, Craig. I just didn't think—"

"Of course not." He was standing there, obviously waiting for me to...what?

I sat at the table and pulled out my wrapped burger. "How did it go with Glory today?"

He sat across from me. "We're hiring people, and I'll be there days during the week. I'll take nights on the weekends."

"That sounds reasonable. It's going to get very busy there very soon."

"Yes. She told me. Here's the thing." He cleared his throat and folded his hands in front of him. "I have a huge favor. Amanda is fine about watching the girls, but this is a new place, and we're kind of...isolated, and I know she's not feeling very comfortable about that. So the obvious solution is to stay up in Sam's old apartment Friday and Saturday nights, so the girls will be close and Amanda will feel safe. But, well, can you come with me? To clear out the apartment?"

Sam's apartment.

It was two small rooms over the original bar. About five years ago I finally talked him into a little renovation, so the bathroom stopped being a health department nightmare, and the window in the back didn't leak every time it rained. I hadn't thought about it being empty, having to be cleaned out, but it made sense. And it was a good idea to let the girls stay up there if Craig was working nights.

I took a bite of my burger and a sip of sweet tea.

There were so many memories there. That was his *place*, where all the special things in his life were kept, carefully, almost like a shrine. His bookshelf held awards from the Chamber of Commerce in addition to his collection of hardcover and paperback books. The walls were lined with framed photos and articles about him and the restaurant. Then there were his first editions, almost fifty prized volumes, collected over the years and kept in a glass-front cabinet.

And his bed, crowded into a corner. There were memories there, too.

"Sure. We can do it Thursday afternoon. No, I guess morning would be better, while the girls are at school. No problem. We can bring his stuff back here, I guess. Maybe make room in the garage. When you move you can take what you want."

He nodded. "Thank you. But are you serious? The garage? Do you have some sort of giant shoehorn somewhere we can use to pack more stuff in there?"

I looked up. His face was completely neutral, but I saw a twinkle in his eye.

"You can't fool me anymore, Craig Ferris. I've already figured out there's a sense of humor there, somewhere."

He nodded solemnly. "True that."

It was after my dinner was done, the paper bag crumpled and thrown away that I went out, calling the dogs, for our evening walk. I loved this time outside with them, hearing their shuffling in the grass, the water lapping against the stones of the seawall, and the moonlight gleaming on the water.

"Jenna."

I nearly jumped a foot. What was he, some sort of ninja? I turned so fast I almost tripped over myself and I stumbled.

His arm went out immediately and he caught me, and when I straightened up, we were so close that, if I had any boobs to speak of, they'd be poking him right in the chest.

"I didn't mean to startle you."

"I keep forgetting there are people around now." I had to tilt my head up, just a little.

"It's so beautiful here," he said softly. "Calm. And quiet."

It was so quiet I could hear our breathing, but as for calm...my heart was racing so fast I thought it would pound right out of my chest. I felt the heat radiating off of his body and knew I should take at least one, or possibly six steps back.

"Listen," I whispered. "Owl."

The soft hoot was back in the woods, away from the water.

Why didn't the friggin' man move back? Had he never heard the phrase *personal space*? Cause he was all up in mine.

"What's that?" he said. It was a chirrup, shrill and angry.

"Raccoon. Frustrated raccoon. Trying to get into the trash." At that, I stepped back. I had to, or I would have probably done something totally stupid, like run my hands up into his hair, down his chest, around to his butt...

Oh crap. This was Sam's *son*.

Finn came racing up, and I could see by the faint moonlight he had another tree frog in his mouth. I cleared my throat. "You came out here for something?"

"Yes." His voice was hoarse. "Yes. Amanda said you were going to help her with her room? Ferns? What was the name of the place you told her to go?"

"Del's. Just up the highway."

"Good. That's what I needed."

"Glad I could help."

"Thanks. Goodnight."

I stayed out there alone for so long that Chloe actually whined at me.

What the hell was *that*, anyway?

I texted Terri on my first break the next morning.

Having unclean thoughts about my stepson

And ur surprised?

Sometimes, the woman was no help at all.

Later, I got a text from Craig.

Would you like us to save u dinner? Spaghetti&meatballs

God, was he going to start being really nice now? Luckily, it was Buck A Beer night, a perfect excuse to come home late and go straight to bed.

Plans but thanx

My supervisor snagged me in the break room. "How's that son thing working out?"

I sighed. "He's got three daughters, we're all managing fine, but it's only been six days."

"Is he planning to stay there?"

I shook my head. "No. He needs to find a job, he wants to sell the bar...it's very temporary."

She patted my arm. "I'm sure you'll make the best of it, Jenna. You're the one person I know who can always look at any situation, figure out the right thing to do, and then do it, no matter how hard it is."

I smiled in thanks, but felt my stomach roiling. This particular situation had me wanting to do things that were anything but right. I had absolutely no idea why I was having all those very intense feelings about Craig. I put it down to the fact that he was a very attractive man who looked like the man I'd had great sex with for a long time, and I hadn't seen any action in two years, eight months and thirteen days. I put it all down to pure lust.

But with that lust came a twinge of discomfort. Sam's son. As in, the son of the man I'd been married to. What was that? I wasn't big on the Bible, but I had a feeling there was something in there about this sort of thing, and it probably wasn't a good thing.

I swear that everyone at DeeDee and Jack's was waiting for me, even the group of old regulars that sat in the opposite corner and barely nodded. The noise level dropped considerably as I walked in.

I put my hands on my hips and growled. "What? Is my hair green? Is there a giant zit on my nose? *What?*"

"Hell, Jenna," somebody called. "Don't get mad. You know what a big deal this is."

Laughter erupted, and I slouched over to my regular table.

Terri raised her eyebrows. "And?"

"Stop," I muttered.

Karen, halfway through a crab cake sandwich, stopped mid-swallow. "What's going on?"

Terri looked skyward. "Guess who's got the hots?"

"We are not," I said distinctly, "having the hots."

"Well if you *are*," Karen said. "go for it."

Terri leaned in. "If you are, isn't it all a bit...icky? I mean, he's Sam's son. That makes you his...stepmother?"

Stella, who had been sitting quietly at the end of the table, tapped her fork against her glass. "Terri, you make it sound as though she *raised* him. There's no relationship there."

I sighed. "But it crossed my mind."

DeeDee brought my beer. "Menu?" she asked.

I shook my head. "Nope. Clam strips and fries. Extra tartar."

"He looks just like Sam?" she asked, making no move to put in my order, which, I had to say, was annoying.

I nodded and sipped the foam off the top on my beer. "Yes. But the total opposite, personality wise. Although he does have a sense of humor, buried *very* deep."

She folded her arms under her bosom. "Heard the girls were cute."

"They are. DeeDee? I'm kinda starving here."

"Glory tried to poach Miranda."

Miranda was one of DeeDee's best waitresses. "Summer's coming. You know how it gets."

"Yeah? Well, tell her to keep her claws off my staff."

"I will. I promise. As soon as I eat."

"Charlie was here. He's not happy with working so many nights."

"Maybe he can work here? And serve me my dinner?"

She turned abruptly and left.

Karen kicked me under the table. "Jenna, are you kidding? He hasn't even been here a week, and *already*?"

I put my elbows on the table and rested my forehead against my palms. "I just had a very strong physical reaction. Perfectly natural. He's a good looking guy and I haven't had sex in... a while." I dropped my hands and glared at Terri. " But you're right. He's Sam's son, and totally off-limits. So you can stop now."

She spread her hands wide. "Stop what?"

"I know you. You're already picking out bridesmaids dresses. You do that every time I look twice at a man. You are the most marriage-minded woman I've ever met."

Karen nodded in agreement. "She's right, Terri. You want everyone you meet to live happily ever after."

"And right now," I said, "I'd be much happier if I could have my house back. The sooner the better."

Stella cleared her throat. We all turned and looked at her. "Tyrell says Amanda has been cutting, Jenna."

I put down my beer very slowly.

"Not lately, he doesn't think," she went on. "But he saw her scars."

"But she's so sweet," Terri whispered.

Stella shrugged. "Sweet has nothing to do with it, Terri. Even sweet kids feel angry."

"I'm sure Craig knows," I said. "He seems very aware of her and what she's feeling, but thanks for telling me. What else did Tyrell say?"

Stella sighed. "That she's very shy and seems afraid of everyone."

"Yeah," I said.

Stella pointed her finger at me. "You need to find something that she's passionate about, Jenna. Find out what she loves—music or art or animals—anything to connect with her."

"Listen, Stella, I get that she needs guidance, but she's going to be moving away. Craig has said that he is not staying here. I don't know if I want to invest too much."

Stella slammed the palm of her hand on the table, making the cutlery jump. "She is Sam's grandbaby, Jenna."

I glared. "I know that."

"And her mamma died, and she had to leave her home, and she's at risk. Craig is not going to be finding a job tomorrow. He could be here for months. Are you going to help her or not?"

Months? Please, no. Not months. But Amanda, she of sad eyes and drawn in mouth...

"Yes. Of course."

Stella looked happy and a bit smug. "Good girl. Just don't go screwing things up by sleeping with her daddy."

I covered my face with both hands. "Why do I know you people? I should sleep with him. I can't sleep with him. I need to fix his daughter...you all drive me crazy."

Karen kicked me again and I dropped my hands.

She was grinning. "You love us."

"I hate you all."

"No, you don't," Stella said. "You love us and would curl up and die without us."

She was right. As usual.

That night I managed to sneak into the house without seeing Craig at all and spent the entire next day at work trying to figure out how I could spend the rest of my life without ever being alone in the same room with him again. When I wasn't thinking about that, I was imagining him naked.

I was a little conflicted about my feelings for him.

When I thought about it rationally, I knew that my attraction to him was based largely on the fact that he was just as handsome as his father had been. I recognized that it was a pretty creepy reason to want to have sex with someone, but, there it was. But even if I'd never met a man named Sam Ferris, Craig would have *still* ticked off all my boxes. I'd gone to bed with men who were less appealing, and whom I'd known for a lot less time. In fact, there was a time in my life when the one night stand was my go-to form of recreation. When I hit thirty, I recognized the behavior as rather self-destructive and I'd become more selective. And the last person I'd slept with had been Sam.

I checked with HR on my break. I had three weeks vacation due. Maybe I could just leave town for a while, go someplace tropic and forget all about Craig and his broad shoulders and big, brown eyes, his moppet twins, and the sad-eyed Amanda. I could drink fruity things with umbrellas in them, and dance to calypso music with sexy younger men. Or older men. I wasn't that picky. Maybe I could scratch this itch with some guy I'd never see again, so that when I got back, Craig would stop being a temptation. Better yet, when I got back he'd have found a job in Norfolk and moved into a nice, big house across the Bay.

Or maybe when I got back he'd race out the front door to meet me, tell me how much he'd missed me, and we'd have the best sex ever right there on the front porch.

I got a text. *Stuffed pork chops tonight. Can we save u a plate?*

The man was relentless. What, no tofurkey with quinoa and kale? He had to make stuffed pork chops?

Yes,thanx. C u later

I texted Terri. *Can u go on vacation with me to an island somewhere? As soon as I'm done renovating the Farnham place and have secured the love and devotion of Steve McCann.*

So, I'd go alone.

When I got home, Maddie and Larissa were at the dining table, workbooks open. Bit was on the chair next to Maddie. Finn and Chloe were under the table. Finn lifted his head and wagged his tail. Chloe woofed gently. Bit ignored me completely, obviously forgetting that I'd rescued her from a fate worse than death—the Northampton County Animal Shelter—and brought her to the doggy equivalent of a Sandals Resort.

"Where's your dad?" I asked.

Maddie looked up. "With Amanda. She had a bad day."

"Someone made her cry."

"No, she hit someone and made *them* cry."

"No, *she* got hit."

I dropped my purse on the table and practically ran down the hallway.

Amanda's door was open, and Craig was lying on the bed, Amanda curled up beside him. They were talking, very quietly, and it was obvious she'd been crying.

I stopped in the doorway and watched as Craig gently pushed the hair from her face, whispering, and she nodded her head against his chest.

"Hey. You guys need anything?"

He looked up and shook his head briefly. "No thanks Jenna. I think we're good now."

Amanda pushed herself up and off of Craig, wiping her eyes with the back of her hand. "Look. We bought these last night. I wanted you to come with us, but Daddy said you were busy. Are these good?"

She pointed to three pretty blue glazed pots in the corner.

I entered her room and walked to where the pots lay, carefully stacked. I crouched down and looked at them closely. I needed a minute to myself, to arrange my face and my thoughts as my heart suddenly burst with pain for this sad, lost girl, crying into her father's shoulder. Why should I care, anyway? But I did. Very much. I swallowed hard and felt myself settle. "These are perfect," I told her, standing. "I'm not working tomorrow, so we can put a few plants in these for you. Do you want to hang them from the ceiling? Or put them on your dresser?"

"How can I hang them up?"

"Easy. I have some rope we can use, we make a few knots, put a hook in the ceiling, and bingo, instant retro sixties chic."

Amanda narrowed her eyes, obviously not getting the reference, but willing to go along. "Okay."

I put my hand on her head. "Good. Now, I'm going to eat a delicious stuffed pork chop. Did you help your dad?"

She shook her head. "No. I wasn't feeling too good when I came home today."

"Oh. Well, I bet they're pretty good, even without your help."

She nodded. "Daddy's a good cook."

I looked over her head at Craig. He looked exhausted, his face pale and sad. "Yes, he is." I left.

I reheated my dinner in the microwave, Maddie and Larissa telling me about their day.

"Holden is a doo-doo head."

"Lunch was good today. Grilled cheese and tomato soup."

"This workbook is too hard to erase in."

"When we got home today, Finn was eating a frog."

"It was so disgusting."

"Can we fish off the dock?"

I took a forkful of pork chop. It was delicious. Why was I not surprised? "I have fishing poles in the garage. I'll try to find them for you guys. Have you fished before?"

"We went out in a boat."

"With Grandpa Rob. In the lake."

"We didn't catch anything."

"He did. A really big fish. But we didn't eat it."

"Do you," I asked cautiously, "have a grandma too?"

"Besides you? Yes, but she and Grandpa Rob are divorced. His new wife is Penny."

"She's pretty young."

"She wants us to live with her, but I don't like her."

"I like Grandpa Rob, though."

"Guys," I said gently, "I'm not really your grandma. I know I was married to Sam, but we were divorced too."

"You'd make a good grandma, 'cept you're too young."

"Well," I said, "that's good to hear, I guess."

The workbooks closed and Maddie went into the cabinet and brought out Oreos. She gave one to her sister and took one for herself. She looked at me.

"Daddy says we're only allowed one before bedtime because of all the sugar. Do you want one?"

My plate was empty. "That would be great. Thank you."

She put one Oreo in front of me, and I watched as she and her sister carefully took their cookies apart, scraped away the cream inside, and slowly ate each wafer. When they were done they took up their schoolwork and left, saying goodnight.

I ate my Oreo in one bite and put my plate in the dishwasher.

I took a long shower, changed, and headed back to the living room, turned on the television, and sat as the dogs, without the twins to entertain them, found their places around me. Ghost appeared from nowhere and jumped up behind me, purring loudly.

I heard his footsteps in the hallway halfway through a rerun of *The Big Bang Theory*. Maybe he was doing laundry and would keep on going to the other end of the hall. Maybe he left something in his car. Maybe he wanted an Oreo.

He sat down across from me and let out a long sigh.

"How is she?" I asked, reaching for the remote and turning down the volume.

He nodded. "Kids are cruel. Someone said something about

her not having a mother, made a mean crack, and she lost it. It happened at the end of the day, so I just picked her up a little early." He ran his hands over his face. "She and her mother did not get along. Amanda hated living with her. But after she died..." He shrugged. "It was very hard."

"Sure. Listen, Craig, I hate to pry, but the twins were talking about their other grandfather. What happened there?"

He took a long breath. "He was suing for custody of the girls. We had our first court appearance, and he tried to say I was an unemployed, broke, drunk. Luckily, the letter had just come from Ellis, so I was suddenly a well-off business owner with a statement from my sponsor that I'd been attending meetings regularly. He... didn't take it well. We'd been living in a house that he owned, and he told me I had to get out. Which is why I just packed up the girls and drove here."

"So, is that it?"

He shrugged. "I'm living here now. I think we're safe." He ran his hand through his hair. "I hate to ask, but can I just run out for a bit?"

"Ah, sure. But it's after nine. There aren't a whole lot of places around here for you to go."

"I want to go to a meeting."

"Oh. Right. Sure."

"About tomorrow? Can I meet you at Sam's after I drop off the girls? Say, nine?"

"What?"

"Cleaning out Sam's apartment, remember? Can you still help me?"

I'd forgotten that too. Damn. "Whenever you need me."

"Thanks. I'll tell Amanda where I'm going, but the twins are asleep and she's good for the night."

He got up and walked back down to Amanda's room. I listened as his footsteps went back up the hall and out the front door.

We were going to clean out Sam's apartment. Just he and I.

Damn.

Chapter Seven

To get to Sam's apartment, you had to go through the bar, past the restrooms, through the door that said "No Admittance", past the storeroom and walk-in cooler, and up a flight of stairs so narrow he'd had to bring in his mattress through the second-floor windows using pulleys and ropes and three semi-drunken patrons who volunteered for the job in exchange for free tequila.

The door at the top of the stairs was open when I got there.

Walking in caught me off guard. The flood of memories engulfed me, and all I could do was stand in the middle of the dark, narrow room, trying not to cry.

"Jenna? In front."

The back room had two small windows overlooking the alley. Sam had a table and a refrigerator there, as well as a tall dresser packed with his stuff. Sam liked stuff.

The front room was much different, three floor-to-ceiling windows overlooking Main Street, a battered leather couch, a large flat-screen TV, and his bed in one corner. There were a couple of upholstered chairs with frayed arms and rump-sprung seats. And more bookshelves reaching up and full of things that had mattered to him: framed pictures and articles about the bar, souvenirs of his travels, gifts from friends, shells and pieces of driftwood.

Craig was standing by one of the windows, holding a book, carefully turning the pages. Standing in this space, Sam's space, he was so much like his father my heart almost stopped.

"This is a first edition *The Seven Pillars of Wisdom*. Did he know how valuable this is?"

I had to clear my throat. "He'd had it a long time. I remember when he got it, he was very proud of himself. Claims he stole it from a little old lady who didn't know what she had. He may have been joking, but I wouldn't have put it past him. He probably made it sound like he was doing her a big favor by taking it off her hands."

He looked up at me. "Hey, you okay?"

I nodded. "Sure. I, well, I wasn't expecting...I mean there are lots of memories here."

He closed the book. "So the two of you stayed close?"

I had to keep myself from looking at the bed in the corner. "Yes. We became good friends." I gestured to the TV. "We liked to watch old movies together. He loved the musicals. Fred and Ginger, Gene Kelly, Judy Garland. We'd drink beer and sing along."

"That sounds nice."

"It was. It was great. I always had a good time with your father. Except when he first came back, and I still hated his guts for leaving in the first place. But I got over it." I shrugged. "What do you want to do?"

"Well, for now, strip the bed, clean up a bit, just look around. I don't suppose there's a whole lot that can get the girls in any kind of trouble."

I went over to the table beside the bed and opened it. "Well, you might want to take Sam's stash. And his rolling papers, and water pipe. And he had a small porn collection in that cabinet by the TV. And there's a revolver here somewhere...maybe in the back room."

Craig's mouth dropped open. "His stash? And porn?"

I chuckled. "Your father was a child of the sixties. Well, the seventies anyway. He smoked a pipe when he was younger and gave it up, but he never gave up his cigars or his pot. And as for the porn...I believe he used to call them classics. I never watched with him, but he insisted they were very well done."

Craig raised his eyebrows. "Wow. Okay then, I guess I didn't know him all that well after all."

I felt a sudden surge of anger. "We didn't know him at all, Craig. He kept too many secrets. You can't really know a person who keeps half of their life hidden away."

"But you loved him."

The anger fell away as quickly as it came, and I felt tears. "With all my heart. He ruined me for other men. He was...*more* than most men. Smarter and funnier, more curious. When he found something he liked, he went after it with everything he had. It was all or nothing with Sam. His collections became obsessions. When he cooked, there would be eight courses. When he went on a bender, he'd be still knocking down shots at dawn. When he made love to me, he wouldn't let me leave the bed, wouldn't let me sleep. For hours." I stopped abruptly. I hadn't meant to say that much. That had been just between Sam and I, those long and passionate nights together, and I was angry with myself for letting anyone, especially Sam's son, even a glimpse of what we'd shared. I sniffed and closed my eyes. "I'm going to miss him forever."

My shoulders started to shake, and I felt his arms around me, gentle, just holding me as I cried, big, ugly gulping sobs. I allowed myself those few moments, feeling the solid warmth and comfort of his body against mine, then pushed him away. "I'm sorry. I'm sorry. It's just being here."

"I understand. You're right. He was larger than life. I'm going to miss him, too."

I wiped away the tears with trembling fingers. "I don't know why I'm so emotional. Let's get to work. Now, what do you want to keep?"

He ran his hand through his hair. "Well, all the first editions, I guess. I'd like to pack them up and get them out to the house. And these." He crossed over to the bookshelf and picked up a framed article from several years ago, naming Sam's on Main one of the ten best eateries on the Delmarva Peninsula. "Shouldn't these be hung up downstairs? Maybe on the restaurant side?"

"I'd run that by Glory first."

He raised his eyebrows. "True that. I'm running *everything* past Glory. I've got some boxes in the car. Let me bring them up."

"Okay. What about his clothes? Donate? I know there are some of those giant black plastic bags here somewhere."

"I spoke to the pastor on Sunday. She said she could use them in the thrift store," he said. "I think that's best, but if you have any other ideas, let me know." Craig was gone.

I took a deep breath. My idea was to leave everything exactly as it was, but that was the squishy side of me, the side that made me do silly emotional things, like cry like a baby when I should have been over all this by now. I found the black bags and opened a dresser drawer, pulling out T-shirts and flannel shirts and stuffing them in the bag. At one point, I found myself holding a Grateful Dead T-shirt, one of his favorites, and thought about keeping it for myself. But did I need a physical reminder of him? Wasn't the house that we'd shared haunted enough by his memory? No. I pushed it in with the rest. If I started saving his things for myself, I'd end up carrying half the apartment back home with me.

Craig came back, carrying a stack of cardboard boxes, went past me and into the living room.

We worked separately for over an hour. I filled three bags, went through the bookshelves and found his gun, unloaded, on top of a pile of National Geographic magazines. I carried it in to the front room, where Craig had packed all his boxes with books. I handed him the revolver without a word.

"What do I do with it?" he asked.

"I'd turn it in to the county sheriff. Explain who you are, what you were doing, and say you found the gun and don't want it."

He took it gingerly and dropped in on the top of a box of books.

"I'm going to take these down to the car and see if I can grab a few more boxes from the bar," he said, and I followed him out, grabbing a huge bag of clothes.

We made three more trips, and I finally sat on the edge of the bed. "I'm done," I told him.

"Glory said she was looking for more boxes."

"Well, have fun with that. As far as I'm concerned, the place is now safe. We got rid of the gun, and the drugs and the porn…"

Craig nodded, looking thoughtful. "True. But what else should we be looking for? A blow-up sex doll?"

I wasn't sure why, but that hit me as very funny, and I started to giggle. "I'm trying to remember if he ever had one of those."

Craig started to smile. "Or maybe a still under the floorboards?"

"Or a portable meth lab?" By now I was laughing. Maybe I was crazy hormonal, but I could not stop. "Plastic explosives?"

He shook his head, laughing. "Plans for a nuclear bomb?" He staggered over to the bed and sat beside me, his shoulders shaking.

I fell back on the bed, eyes squeezed shut. "Blueprints for an underground missile silo?" I was laughing so hard, I could barely get the words out.

"So you're saying he was really an international spy?" he sputtered.

"Oh, God." I opened my eyes, wiping the tears away. "Sam as a spy. Now, there's an idea."

He fell back on the bed. "It's either that or a top-notch criminal mastermind."

I turned my head to look at him. "That would make more sense."

He turned over on his side, propping his head in his hand. "No. Spy. He wasn't the law-breaking type."

I snorted. "You obviously never saw him raging drunk, standing up in a golf cart, using his feet on the steering wheel to avoid running over the flags on the Bay Creek Golf Course."

His smile faltered. "Was he raging drunk a lot?"

I bit my lower lip. "He was an alcoholic. Totally unapologetic and very high functioning. He knew exactly how much he could handle, which is why he could do his job and run the bar. But once in a while, he just let go. He'd do crazy stuff, reckless stuff. Luckily there was always someone with him to keep him from doing real harm."

"You?"

"A few times. His main drinking buddy was Kenny Malcolm. Now, there's a man who could tell you stories."

"I think I'd rather not know."

I sighed. "There would be good stories, too. Sam was a fine man. Just...flawed."

Sam and I had lain like this, talking, not touching, sometimes for hours. Sam would find a topic and just start talking and I'd listen, drinking in every word, because to me there had been no music as sweet as the sound of his voice.

"He and I never talked about drinking," Craig said. "He was glad when I joined AA, but said it wasn't for him. He had his own way of coping, he said."

"Which was not coping at all. He drank beer all night, every night. When he felt the need, he'd open a bottle of scotch and finish it all by himself." I heard the anger in my voice as I stared up at the ceiling. "He always told me it was part of who he was, and I just had to accept it. And I did. But I never understood that part of him. And I hated what it did to him."

"I'm sorry," he said very softly. "You deserved better."

I turned to face him. He looked so sad that something inside me twisted, a small sharp pain. I reached out and touched his cheek.

And then I kissed him. I know that, in my mind, I wanted to comfort this man, who had just spent the past few hours going through a part of his father's life that he'd never imagined. I wanted him to know it was okay to feel sad, to feel regret. And I didn't want him to stop loving Sam just because of what he now knew.

That's what I wanted to do. Instead, the kiss immediately became more, because he was kissing me back, and there was nothing soft or comforting about it.

This was nothing like the flighty fantasies I'd been having about him. This was very real, and I felt a surge of want and heat and needing more. I opened my mouth to him and moved my body against his, and there was a sudden rush, hands moving, bodies turning, and I felt his fingers against my skin as I tugged at the buttons of his shirt, twisting against him, wrapping my leg around his hip...

"Hey, Craig? I found more boxes."

I threw myself away from him, practically falling off the bed, and bounded to my feet. I tugged my T-shirt back down. My hair had fallen from its topknot, and I tried to smooth the wild tangled mess with both hands.

Glory came through the door, carrying a cardboard box in each hand. I glanced back at Craig. He was standing by the window, tucking in his shirt, his back to me.

"I got more," she said, setting them down. "Should I bring them up?"

Craig turned around, shaking his head and looking completely calm. "I'll get them, Glory. Thanks. We're almost done here, anyway. Right Jenna?"

I swallowed hard. "Yes. I, ah, was just on my way out."

Glory put her hands on her broad hips and tilted her head. "You should wear your hair down more often, honey. Makes you look so much prettier. Don't you think so, Craig?"

He stared at me, his eyes expressionless, then nodded. "Yes. I do think so."

"So listen, Craig? I'll drop those bags of clothes down at the church."

He nodded again. "Sounds good. Thanks."

"And I guess I'll see you back at the house. Good. Okay then. Bye." I practically ran out, grabbing my keys off the coffee table, shooting down the stairs, and out into the open air.

Stella looked up as I burst through the door. The store was empty. Thank God.

"What happened?"

I was still shaking. "Craig and I were clearing out some things at Sam's apartment."

She put her arms around me and hugged. "Oh, Jenna, that must have been so hard for you."

"It was awful. I cried and packed up his clothes, and then I kissed Craig."

She dropped her arms and gave me a very hard, cold look. "What?"

"And he kissed me back, and we probably would have had monkey sex right there on Sam's bed if Glory hadn't interrupted."

"Well, thank you, Glory. Are you crazy? Jenna, you do not even know that man, and have you considered the idea that maybe, just maybe, you're seeing Craig as a substitute for Sam?"

"Of course I've considered it," I shot back. "That's why I'm feeling like total crap right now, even as I'm thinking I really wanted to see us both naked."

"Oh, honey, you need to step back and take a really hard look at this situation."

I sagged against her counter. "Stella, I don't know what to do. I was seriously thinking of taking all my vacation, going somewhere very far from here, and hope he'd be gone by the time I got back."

"That sounds like an excellent idea."

"Yeah, except that I only have three weeks, and that doesn't seem like a very suitable timeframe."

"Maybe you could move out?"

I nodded. "Yes, I thought about that, too. But what would I do about the dogs? And the goats? Not to mention my garden, and, Stella, that is my *home*."

She folded her arms around her waist, her fingers drumming against her arm. "He was a willing participant, I gather?"

"Well, yes."

She raised an eyebrow.

"Yes, I kissed him first, but he kissed me *back*."

"Listen, honey, maybe you both need to get laid, and if that's the case, well, fine. You're both adults. But if you're confusing the feelings you had about Sam with feelings for Craig, somebody could get hurt, and I have a feeling that Craig has been hurt enough."

"I *know*."

"Well, it looks like the two of you need to have a serious conversation."

I almost gagged. "You know how I feel about that sort of crap."

"Yes. I also know that for the past twenty years that I've known you, you have not had one healthy, normal romantic relationship with any man. Except, maybe, your ex-husband. Which, I gotta tell you, was not such a good thing for you. Could be having a serious conversation with any of those men, even the totally unsuitable ones like Kenny Malcolm, would have made a difference."

I turned and slid down the front of her counter until I was sitting on the floor, legs straight in front of me. I leaned my head back. "Can I just stay here?"

She shook her head and made a tsk-tsk kind of noise. "No, you may not. You can get up, put on your big girl panties and deal with this like a grown-up. The sooner the better."

"Don't you ever get tired of being right?"

"No."

I saw, from my vantage point on her floor, Craig's Suburban drive down Main Street. He was probably heading for the house, which meant if I followed him, we could be alone and have a serious talk, just the two of us, and figure out what had just happened between us and decide what to do about it.

Or maybe, I could just follow him onto the house, take off all my clothes, and surprise him while he was sorting first editions.

"This is hard," I wailed.

"Life is hard," Stella said. "Get your skinny ass off my floor and go live it."

When I got to the house, the back of the Suburban was up. I got out, grabbed a box of books, and carried it in the house.

He was sitting in the living room, just sitting there, looking down at the box he'd carried in. Finn jumped off the couch and came over to say hello, but I didn't even pet him. I dropped the box, and Craig jumped, looked at me, and looked away.

"Look, I'm really sorry," I began. "That was a mis—"

"It won't happen again," he said woodenly. He still didn't look at me. He was staring at the floor. "It was an emotional place for the both of us. I'm sure you were feeling vulnerable, and missing him, and I was a very handy substitute."

I started to shake my head. "No, Craig—"

"I get it, and it's fine but it's over." He finally lifted his eyes and looked at me. I felt my stomach start to churn, seeing the anger and the hurt there.

"That's not what that was about," I said. "And you *did* kiss me back."

"You're an attractive woman," he said coldly. "But it won't happen again. You were my father's wife."

There was silence. Finn paced back and forth between us, his nails making little tapping noises on the floor.

Okay I got it. It was awkward, and maybe embarrassing, but did he really have to be such a total dick about it? I clenched my jaw. I had a bad habit of saying exactly what was on my mind, and had discovered, the hard way, that sometimes I was better off not saying anything at all. Right now, I wanted to tell him that even though he looked like his father, he was very much *not* like him at all, and that whatever caused me to kiss him in the first place was not just about looking for him to take Sam's place. I wanted to tell him that I liked *him*, even though he was a little too serious for my taste, and I respected the job he was doing as a single dad. I wanted to tell him that I didn't mind him and his daughters at the house at all. In fact, I was almost getting used to them, even if it *did* mean I couldn't walk around in my underwear anymore.

I wanted to tell him that I didn't care why I kissed him, but I really wanted to do it again, and could we please just be two consenting adults, take our clothes off and see what happened?

But I didn't say any of that, because the little niggling I had in the back of my mind about his being Sam's son had also taken hold in *his* mind. I was the ex-wife of his father. That made things... complicated. More than complicated. Probably impossible.

I changed tracks. "Have you looked for a job yet?"

"Actually, yes. I spoke to a headhunter yesterday. I have to polish up my resume and get it to her."

More silence. "Well," I said at last. "I'm glad we got that straightened out." I pushed the box of books toward him with my foot. "Just put these on my bookshelf, there's plenty of space along the bottom there. I have those clothes in my car. I'll drop them off at the church, and then I'm going across the Bay to do some shopping. I'll be back late tonight."

"Amanda thinks you'll be here."

Well...poop. "Then I'll come back this afternoon and head across the bridge after we're done."

He dropped his eyes again. "Thank you. She...counts on people keeping their word. It's important to her."

"I'll keep my word," I told him, and left.

I stopped to speak with my neighbor, Dave, on my way back from the church.

Dave was at least seventy, possibly older. No one knew for sure, and he wasn't much for sharing. He was born in Eastville and had been on his little place right on the Bay for as long as I could remember, and when Sam and I had first bought the house, we barely saw him at all. He had a huge garden, chickens, kept bees, and lived, as they say now, off the grid. The solar panels on his roof had been replaced twice in the years I'd known him, and he had a wood burning stove for heat. His pride and joy was an ancient Ford pickup that he kept in tip-top condition. Over the years, we'd built a quiet, tentative friendship. When our section of Eastville had been rezoned, and my taxes jumped through the roof, it was he who suggested I keep goats and call myself a farm. When I asked him what I would do with goats, he laughed, and said he'd take care of that.

And he did. He milked the goats and made sweet, creamy cheese that he sold in town. I knew he was a veteran and had been blinded in one eye, so he probably collected a government pension. He always said he didn't care much for money, he had all he really needed, and I believed him. He was happy and self-sufficient.

He lived in a three-room ranch with an attached garage and workshop. He was out in his garden when I drove up, and he showed me what he'd put in. His was a garden that needed to feed him all year round, with plenty extra to sell at the weekly farmer's market that ran all summer. He may not have cared for money, but still needed it to pay for the repairs on his beloved truck.

He offered me honey and fresh eggs. I gave him the local news. We drank sweet tea sitting on his bench, right on the water. He had clam beds out there, and I had often waded in with him, raking the bottom, then feasting on fresh clams opened straight from the water, flavored by the bay and a squirt of lemon juice. I worried about his health and occasionally talked him into my taking his blood pressure and listening to his heart. He hadn't seen a doctor, he told me, in thirty years.

I glanced at the clock on my phone. I still had an hour before Amanda would be home. I figured I was safe from Craig. He was probably in town, or at least on his way to pick up the twins from the bus stop.

Dave rose slowly and walked me to my Jeep. He rubbed the hood, buffing out a smudge, and looked at me keenly from his one dark eye.

"Them's children at your place now? Who do they belong to?"

"Sam's grandkids, Dave. Sam had a son. I never knew."

He nodded thoughtfully. "From that New York woman?"

I froze. "He talked to you about her?"

Dave nodded, is short gray hair gleaming silver in the sun. "He'd come over sometimes. Get drunk. I figgered he talked to me 'cause he knew I wouldn't be talkin' to nobody else."

I leaned against the Jeep. "What did he say?"

Dave shrugged. "Just that he'd loved a New York woman. Loved her fierce. Wanted to marry her, but she said no. After you divorced, he tole me she gave him a son. Was pleased by that, Sam was."

I didn't know what to say. I knew that Sam and Dave spent time drinking, and I was pretty sure that Dave grew marijuana in an overgrown field out in the woods, which was where Sam got his stash. It made sense that Dave would be the one person to keep Sam's secrets.

I got back home and the Suburban was gone. I left the honey and eggs on the kitchen counter, and went out to look at my potted ferns.

Sam had built a sunroom off the living room that ran across the back half of the house. Since it faced south, it stayed fairly comfortable in the winter, and in the summer, the shade from all the trees kept it from being unbearably hot. I rarely used it except as another place to put things, mostly my outdoor plants, to keep them alive thru the winter. I had a bench full of ferns and four palm trees that I was planning to put out around the dock.

Today was as good a day as any.

I was in my garden when they got back, and I saw Amanda running up, her backpack draped over one shoulder, her thin face smiling.

"You remembered!"

"Your dad reminded me. Bring out your pots, and we'll see what we can do."

She came out a few minutes later, carrying the largest pot, Maddie and Larissa trailing behind, each holding another pot.

"Are those eggs from real chickens?"

"Is that honey from the beehives we saw?"

"Did you put the palm trees on the dock today?"

"Can we put white lights on them?"

"I can see strawberries on the plants! Can we eat them yet?"

"The beans are sprouting. How long before they grow up?"

Craig brought up the rear. "Do you need help with anything?" His voice was pleasant and he looked relaxed, nothing at all like the tense and angry man I'd left a few hours earlier.

"I think we're good," I said. I saw Maddie crouched by one of the beds, her little hand reaching for a tender sprout. I didn't want anyone trampling my garden. And I wanted Amanda and I to spend some time quietly, just the two of us. She was worming her way, very slowly, into my thinking. Every time I looked into that little girl's eyes, I wanted to hug the sadness away. "Why don't you three walk the goats while Amanda and I take care of these ferns?"

Maddie's jumped up and she and Larissa were off and running.

Craig's mouth twitched. "Walk the goats?"

"The girls will show you. Just please, don't let any of them loose, or I'll be out here all night trying to round them back up."

"Okay."

I looked at Amanda, who was smiling shyly. "Thank you," she said softly.

"Well, we didn't need them, and your dad looked like he could use some exercise."

She poked one of the ferns with a thin finger. "Yeah, he wasn't in such a good mood today."

"How about you? Was today better?"

She nodded. "Yes. Tyrell introduced me to his cousin, Keesha, and she and I had lunch together. She's nice."

I didn't know Keesha, but Stella had five children of her own, and six sisters, and her family was spread all across Northampton County.

"It's good to have a friend," I said.

"Yes."

We started by dividing the ferns. Over the winter, they had gone fairly dormant, but by this time of the year, the root balls were dense and new shoots were sprouting everywhere. I did the heavier lifting, cutting through the root balls and shaking away the excess dirt. Amanda sat on the ground at my feet, in easy reach of the large garbage can where I kept my garden soil. She planted the sections carefully, tamping down the dirt, until all three pots were ready. I showed her how to mix water and Epsom salts in a large galvanized bucket, and we submerged each pot for five minutes, then pulled it up and put it on the worktable, letting the excess water drain away.

"Do this every week," I told her. "They'll stay beautiful and green. I'll help you until you get used to it, okay?"

She was smiling, and her thin face was transformed. I saw nothing of Craig in her at all. She must have looked exactly like her mother.

We heard the twins coming back just as we were finishing up. Craig was walking between his daughters, and each of them was holding a hand. He was laughing, and looked happy and totally relaxed. He'd walk a few steps, then lift up one of the girls by her arm, and she'd hang there, screaming and giggling until he let her down. I watched him, and started to laugh. The girls were so obviously enjoying themselves, despite their screams of protest. I wondered how he had the strength to keep lifting them one after the other, and then quite suddenly, one of the little girls twisted away, and started to scream in such a way that I knew something had gone very wrong.

Chapter Eight

It was Maddie, and she sat, holding her elbow, and screaming, her eyes squeezed shut. Craig was on his knees and looked stricken. Larissa, standing behind her father, started crying.

I dropped down beside Maddie and looked at her arm. She was holding it out stiffly, her little fingers clenched around her elbow.

Craig stood up. "I'll call 911," he said.

I looked up at him. "I know what this is, Craig. Don't call, she's fine."

"No, she's not," he roared. "I pulled her arm off." There was fear in his face and in his voice, and Amanda started to whimper.

"No, Craig, you didn't. Listen to me. This is my job. You can call 911, wait for an ambulance to take her up to the MedCenter half an hour away, or you can let me fix this right now. This is called nursemaids elbow. It happens all the time to little kids, and I can take care of this now if you let me."

He was breathing so fast and so heavily, I was worried he'd hyperventilate.

"Craig, you need to take a deep, slow breath. Right now."

He closed his eyes, then opened them, and I could practically see him fighting down his panic. He glanced down at Larissa, who was wailing, her arms wrapped around his waist.

"Craig?"

He nodded.

I took Maddie's face in both my hands and turned it toward me. "Honey, you need to stop crying for just a second and tell me when it hurts."

"It hurts now," she wailed, eyes still tightly closed.

"Are you sure?"

She sniffed and opened her eyes, looking down at her arm. "I'm afraid to move it."

"Yeah, honey, I know. But let go and let me move it. Please?"

She bit her trembling lower lip, nodded, and unclenched her fingers.

I ran my hands up and down her arm gently. Nothing was broken. "Now, it hurt when you twisted and Daddy was swinging you, right?"

She nodded.

"Okay. I want you to move it, just a little, to see if it hurts again."

Tears started again. "I don't want to."

"I know, honey, but I have to make sure. If it hurts again, I can fix it for you. Otherwise, you have to go to the hospital. Do you want to do that?"

She shook her head, and started to bend her arm. She barely moved it, then stopped. "It hurts," she whined.

"Good." I felt her elbow, watching her little face as my fingers found the right spot. "What I'm going to do," I said, keeping my voice light, "is called a reduction. See, your elbow popped right out of its socket."

Maddie's eyes widened. "It's not even connected?"

I smiled at her. "That's right. Boy, *you* should be the nurse! Now, I have to put your arm back together." I held her wrist. "It's a very special talent," I said. "And it might hurt again for just a second. But sometimes it helps if you count to ten, really, really fast. Come on, we'll do it together."

She was looking at me with absolute trust. "Okay, Jenna.

"Good girl. Now, look right in my eyes, and we'll count. Ready? Onetwothreefour—"

I slipped the elbow joint back in place. She gasped, and for a second I thought she'd start to cry again, but she just looked surprised, then scowled at me.

"You tricked me. You didn't wait until ten!"

I shook my head and put my finger on the tip of her nose. "I never told you I'd *wait* until ten. I just said we should *count* to ten. Can you move your arm now?"

She began to bend it, very slowly. Then, she straightened it back down. "I think it works."

"I think so, too. Come on, baby, get up and give your dad here a hug. I think he needs one pretty badly."

She scrambled up and Craig swept her into his arms, rocking her back and forth.

"You're squishing me," she squealed, kicking.

He let her down gently. "Maddie, I am so sorry. I promise, I will never do that again."

Her little face dropped. "But Daddy, that's so much fun!"

Larissa tugged at her sister's shirt. "Is it better? How much did it hurt? I heard it click, did you?"

Maddie nodded and they started back toward the house, Amanda behind them. "Worse than a bee sting. I *felt* it click. That part didn't hurt."

Craig covered his face with his hands, and when he dropped them, he was still white and trembling. "I thought I pulled her arm out."

"Technically, you did. This happens to kids. Not usually at this age, but it happens. She'll be fine."

He stared at the ground for what seemed to be a very long time before raising his eyes. "Look, I was a real jerk earlier."

I wanted to say, yes, you were, but managed to keep my mouth shut. "It's fine."

"No, it's not." He nodded, as if to himself, a few times before speaking. "We have to live together in that house, and I don't want us to feel like we can't be in the same room together."

Oh? Because you think I'll tear your clothes off? But, again, I actually thought before I spoke. "We're both grown-ups, Craig. We can be nice and polite to each other."

"Yes. Good."

We stood in the fading sunlight, staring at each other. I was acutely aware of the stretch of his denim shirt across his chest, the faint shadow of a beard on his jaw, his dark eyes, narrowed and searching my face.

"We're good, Craig. It's all good."

And I turned and went into the house, leaving him standing on the gravel drive, alone.

We each kept our word. We were nice and polite to each other.

Weeks went by. School ended, and the twins went to the town recreation program every morning. Amanda insisted she was too old for it, but found a perfect solution. She and Keesha volunteered to work with the counselors, so she spent the mornings with her sisters. The days I worked, they walked from the large playground in the center of town back to Main Street for lunch with Craig, and then they spent the day at the beach. Keesha and Amanda were both paid by Craig to babysit. Rainy days were spent in the upstairs apartment, now furnished with a collection of kid-friendly movies for the DVD player and a Wii.

I tried to take the girls on Thursdays. Keesha came with us, as she and Amanda had become BFFs in a very short time. Stella confided in me that Keesha's mom, her sister's youngest, had a drug problem and was currently serving another six-month sentence in jail, leaving Keesha with a strict and loving father who worked two jobs. Keesha had been spending too much time alone. The friendship was saving both little girls.

We went up and down the Delmarva Peninsula, playing tourists. We saw gardens and historical spots, played minigolf and saw the ponies on Chincoteague. I took them to my favorite beaches, the ones the summer people hadn't found that you could only get to by walking through forgotten trails and ducking under old wooden fences.

We had a great time together. I was starting, very slowly, to fall in love with those girls.

Craig was busy. Sam's on Main kicked into high gear, and on the weekend, I never saw him. I had the house to myself, as he and the girls lived in the apartment from Friday night to Monday morning.

I spent that time with my friends. We still had a standing Friday night date, starting at the Grove, then dinner, then ...whatever. The summer people were there in force, and our usual rhythm was thrown off, but we still had each other, the best company in the world. Stella mentioned Dara French, the new doctor in town, just often enough for all of us to start gently teasing her, which she took with her usual good grace. Terri had talked her friend Chris into buying the little house on Main Street.

"It's been gutted," Terri explained. "Chris and I will be able to do anything we want in there. And I've already talked to the McCann brothers and they're going to help us."

Stella looked confused. "Did she come down and look at it?"

Terri shook her head. "No. She trusts me. I had power of attorney and she wired funds to Ellis. She'll be down in a few weeks."

After that, she mentioned Steve McCann at least once every half hour, which was tiresome, but after Karen started openly keeping count, Terri got her enthusiasm under control. I signed up for Karen's Saturday yoga class, which started about an hour after our weekly breakfast ended. She and I walked back to her studio, talking. She knew more about my feelings for Craig than any of them, and listened without judgment. Her class was fun, lots of summer people, but it was as much for something to do as it was for the actual class. I found that without Craig and the girls around, the house was a little too quiet.

I knew he'd found a regular meeting to go to every Tuesday morning. He had one day off, Wednesday, and he spent the time with his daughters at the house. Amanda's furniture got painted, the carpeting was pulled up and the wooden floors buffed. He bought a canoe and paddled all the way up Logan's Creek. Maddie and Larissa both complained bitterly that they never went out into the Bay, but Craig knew that the water out there was tricky, and there were currents and sudden gusts that could easily overturn a small canoe.

"But we can swim."

"We always wear out life vests."

"I want to see dolphins."

"There aren't any dolphins."

"Yes, there are! And sharks!"

"Will you take us?"

I shook my head firmly. "No. I absolutely will not."

The few evenings we did spend together moved past the atmosphere of an armed truce to mutual surrender. We talked, even laughed. We watched old movies. He helped with some things around the house. I knew he'd gone on two interviews, but hadn't heard back. Olivia Kopecknie had asked him, twice, to dinner, but he declined. When he mentioned it, very briefly, I felt something in my chest, a tightening, then release, and that's when I realized that it wasn't just lust anymore. As much as I still wanted to sleep with Craig Ferris, I also wanted something else.

It wasn't anything like what I had felt for Sam, because beyond the physical resemblance, Craig was a completely different man. He was cautious and steady, whereas Sam did anything he wanted on a whim. Craig looked at the world as a father, thinking what was best for his family, and that gave him a selflessness that Sam would never have understood. Sam had always been for Sam first, last, and always. And even though I knew he loved me as much as he loved anyone, he had never put me first.

There was no wide-eyed adoration. I didn't hold my breath until he walked through the door. I didn't hang on his every word. I was a middle-aged woman now, not a headstrong young girl who wanted everything and felt she deserved it all. I knew now that love needed to be earned and treasured. I knew that loving someone came at a cost and could never be taken for granted.

I felt a deep, almost painful longing for him and his company. I was completely happy just sitting in the same room with him. My heart almost burst into flames every time he smiled. As much as I ached to touch him, I kept a careful and controlled distance. I was terrified that if I let myself slip, I'd do something to drive him away.

When I told my sister, she was very quiet. During the summer, Virginia Beach was block after block of traffic, and we didn't go down to walk on the beach. Instead, we'd sit on the balcony, squinting at the water from the small shady perch.

"Does he know?" she asked.

I shook my head. "How could he? I've been on my best behavior."

"Maybe you should try a little misbehaving?"

"No."

"Or you could just tell him?"

"No."

"Because?"

She was in a relationship now, the gentleman who had made her go woo-woo. I'd met him, a quiet man with a sweet smile only for my sister. "This isn't like you and Simon," I said.

"Why not?"

"Because the two of you met with intent. You were both looking for someone. Craig wasn't looking for anything when he came down here, and what he got was a crazy redhead who kissed him on his father's bed."

"But you feel different now. Just tell him."

I shook my head. "To what end? He's looking for a job. He's had interviews. Somebody is going to hire him. Maybe he'll move to Baltimore or Richmond. Who knows where he'll go? But he'll leave."

"If you love him, maybe he'll stay."

"No. If he loved *me* maybe he'd stay. And that hasn't happened. And there's this thing about me being Sam's wife. It's..."

"It's ridiculous, that's what it is. You have no previous relationship with him, Jenna. In fact, you never knew of his existence."

I shrugged. "I know. But he mentioned it, and he's not the kind of guy to just say things for the sake of talking, you know? It obviously weighs on his mind."

She grabbed my hand. "I'm sorry, baby sister."

"Me too."

On a Friday night at the end of June, Terri brought her friend to the Grove.

"She just drove down this second," Terri explained, grinning. "She's staying with me, and tomorrow she's seeing the house for the first time. Want to meet us?"

I smiled. Terri's happiness was infectious. "Sure. But Chris, you haven't seen the house at all? And you let Terri buy it for you?"

Chris, a tiny woman with a riot of curls that fell past her shoulders, was dressed in a short linen dress and flip-flops. She was olive-skinned, had big dark eyes and a decidedly Roman nose. "I saw the pictures on Zillow," she said.

Terri gave Chris a big squeeze. "We're going to have so much fun!"

Karen shook her head at Chris "You let her talk you into this?"

Chris shrugged her shoulders. "I really needed the change, and I was swayed by the promise of hot men."

"And you believed Terri?" I asked, still smiling

She smiled, her teeth small and very white. "I've known her along time, so I've learned to sift out the BS. I really just want to live somewhere I can walk to both the water and at least one bar."

"Well, then your new place is perfect," I said.

She rolled her eyes. "Not yet, but I see potential."

We had dinner at Shorty's then went down to Sam's on Main. Craig was in the restaurant side, so I just popped my head in and gave him a wave.

Chris, who followed me in, poked me in the ribs. "See, sometimes Terri tells the truth."

Craig looked up, saw me, and nodded briefly. Then he looked past me, and his face changed. He'd seen Chris. I glanced at her, and she broke into a smile.

"Who is *that*?" she asked.

Terri grabbed Chris's arm and shook her head. "He's taken."

"No," I said distinctly, "he's not." I looked at Chris. "That's Craig Ferris. He owns Sam's now. He's got three girls."

Chris was still smiling. "Not a problem."

"But he's taken," Terri said again. She glared at me, and we went back into the bar. We didn't stay long and went further down Main Street to Bogey's. Chris, knocking back tequila shots, pointed happily down Main. "See? I'm going to be living right there. Close to everything."

"Including all this crowd walking past your house day and night," Karen said. "You'll have drunks puking on your front lawn all summer."

Chris stopped looking happy. "Really?" she asked.

"It's crazy here," Stella told her. "Summer is crazy. Like Rehoboth. But it's worth it for the rest of the year."

Chris sighed. "Too late now," she said, and took another shot.

The next morning, I drove down the alley that ran parallel to Main and pulled in behind Chris's new house. The backyard was a disaster. The porch had completely come apart from the main house, and looked to be hanging on by one nail. All the windows had been boarded up and the paint was peeling off in large curlicues.

I walked around to the front. The door was locked with a padlock. I stepped away from the house and stood on the sidewalk, giving it a long, hard look.

It had been built as a summer cottage, with a broad front porch and pitched roof. The windows across the front were all cracked. The porch roof sagged and the walkway from the sidewalk to the porch was in pieces.

Early morning traffic wasn't bad down Main Street going toward the beach, but it was only ten o'clock. I knew that by noon the cars would be bumper to bumper. I looked down the street and sure enough, Terri and Chris were hurrying down the sidewalk.

"Only six minutes from my condo to here," Terri informed me. "I'm so excited." She took a key out of the pocket of her linen shorts and unlocked the padlock, pushed the door open, and spread her arm out, waving Chris inside. "Your castle awaits."

Chris stepped forward, then stopped abruptly. "Terri," Chris said softly, "where's the floor?"

I looked over Chris's shoulder.

Obviously, someone had been in the process of some sort of renovation. Terri had not exaggerated. The place was stripped down to the studs, including the floor. There wasn't even subflooring. The floor was nothing but joists, and you could look directly down into the stone crawlspace underneath. There were plywood strips, a foot wide, placed on top of the joists, creating a path of sorts to the back of the house.

Terri put her arm around her friends' shoulder. "We have a blank slate," she said.

Chris took a tentative few steps onto the plywood, Terri and I cautiously following. "Did you know it looked like this?" Chris asked, incredulous. "Because the pictures..."

"Well, see the pictures on Zillow were a few years old," Terri explained brightly. "It had been put on the market three years ago, hadn't sold, so the owner started to redo the place, but didn't get too far."

"So you knew there was no floor?" Chris asked.

"Of course I did," Terri responded, sounding hurt and surprised. "You don't think I'd let you buy something without my even *looking* at it."

"And," Chris continued, "you opened the door, saw this, and decided it was just perfect for me?"

"Chris, I told you we'd be starting from scratch. What did you think I meant? Besides, the location is ideal. I had Mike McCann look at the place, and he said the walls and rafters are sound, and the foundation will last another hundred years. There's even a yard out back, once you cut down all the weeds and saplings. And get rid of the old tires. The point is, we can do whatever we want here."

I cautiously stepped over a few joists, got back on the plywood, and started poking around. "All of the windows are either boarded up or cracked single pane. You'll have to replace them all. The plumbing looks at least fifty years old and the electric is knob and tube, " I told them.

"What does that mean?" Terri asked.

"It means it has to go. I thought you watched HGTV," Chris said.

"The good news is," I told them, " you can see all the beams here, and it doesn't look like you've got any termites."

"Of course not," Chris muttered. "There's not enough wood for them to eat."

"There's lots of room, Chris," Terri said. "And you could have really tall ceilings." She pushed her friend further into the empty space, and spread her arms. "Open concept, yes? The kitchen along that wall, the dining room in that little bay window."

"There's no window," Chris pointed out.

"No," Terri agreed, "but there will be. All we need to do is add the glass. Two bedrooms and a shared bathroom right in the back. We'll move the back door to the side and have a nice brick path to the yard. The driveway comes right up to the house from the alley, so we can put in a carport if you like, and a covered patio."

"There's no floor," Chris repeated. "How can I live in a house with no floor?"

"You're staying with me for as long as it takes," Terri said brightly. "We'll have so much fun. And every day, you can walk down here and watch them work. And I'm taking my vacation in a few weeks, and I'm staying right here in Cape Edwards to help you out."

Chris glared. "You're staying right here in Cape Edwards so you can snag a McCloud brother."

"No, honey," Terri said. "Not McCloud. That was Dennis Weaver. *McCann.*"

I patted Chris on the back. "Welcome to the neighborhood," I told her.

We had made our way to the back of the house where all the windows had been boarded up and there was little light, so the house looked a lot less of a mess than it probably was.

Chris shook her head. "Terri, this is way more work than I imagined. How are we going to do this?"

On cue, a voice boomed out from the front door. "Hey, Terri. It's Steve McCann."

Even in the dark gloom, I could see Terri blush. So could Chris, who rolled her eyes and carefully made her way back to the front.

Steve McCann had been ahead off me in school, but I'd known him all my life. He saw me and nodded a greeting.

"Hey, Red, are you in on this too?"

I shook my head. "Nope. Just an innocent bystander."

Chris stuck out her hand, and Steve shook it. "I'm Chris Polittano. I'm the official owner. Terri says you're a miracle worker."

Steve was tall and lanky. He'd played basketball in high school, and he still moved with a certain grace. His face was all angles: high cheekbones, firm jawline, a thin nose. He was a good looking man, and being a successful businessman made him one of Cape Edwards' prize catches. I'd never looked at him that way, because I'd known him for so long and remembered him as the cocky jerk who used his brief stardom on the basketball court to sleep with as many girls as he could get into the back of his Mustang convertible. He'd been five years ahead of me in school, but every girl in the district knew all about Steve McCann.

"Well," said Mike, coming up behind his brother. "Maybe small miracles."

Mike was older, and I didn't know him at all, but he was also a handsome man, shorter than his brother, with a barrel chest and twinkling blue eyes, graying hair and a short, dark beard.

"I'm Mike," he said, taking Chris' hand. "And this here is Steve, and I promise you, we will make this place look like a dream."

Chris looked from one to the other, and I could see her face soften. Terri's promise had just come true, and I could see a smile start to tug at her mouth. "Walk me through it," she challenged.

"Later guys," I said, and made my way back outside.

I walked down to Sam's on Main and picked up the girls. Sam was in the tiny back office, the door closed, but I stuck my head in to tell him we were going. He looked up briefly and nodded. We went back to the house and worked in the garden. Amanda helped me weed. Every year, right before the Fourth of July, the vegetables started ripening so thick and fast I could barely keep up. Then we all went fishing off the dock. I'd caught rockfish and striped bass in the past. Today, we caught nothing, but we tied chicken wings to the big crab trap I had pulled out of the garage and threw it in. If we were lucky, there would be fresh crab for dinner tomorrow night.

I brought them back around eight. The restaurant was packed, as was the bar. I hurried them upstairs, supervised showers, popped a movie in the DVD player and made my way downstairs.

I met Craig halfway up the staircase.

It was a narrow enough space and dimly lit. He was two steps below me, and our eyes were level.

"They're clean and sleepy," I told him.

He looked exhausted and slumped against the wall of the stairwell. "Thank you so much. When you told me the summer would be busy, I never imagined..."

"Yeah," I said. "The good news is it's only three months."

"Sure. But there's two months to go. I may not make it."

I grinned and poked his shoulder. "What, a big strong guy like you? Remember, your father did it, and he had twenty years on you."

"True. But I believe he was fueled by booze and various chemicals."

"No chemicals. All natural."

He chuckled. "Right. I forgot how health-conscious he was."

We stood without speaking, but the air between us crackled. Maybe it was the hot summer night. Maybe it was my own body, sweating in a loose linen dress. Maybe it was the music, coming up from the bar, but I knew that all he had to do was lean forward and touch me, and I would explode. Surely, I thought, this wasn't just me. He had to feel it, too.

He dropped his eyes and backed down the stairs, letting me walk down and past him. Our bodies never touched.

"Thanks again," he said.

"Sure." I didn't turn around. I just kept walking, through the storeroom, into the bar, and out into the night.

It was Karen's birthday, and she sent me a text.

Celebrating at the pier. Michigan Zydeco. I know you just got off work but come dance with me.

I read the text just as I got off my shift, and texted her right back.

B there by 9

It was Wednesday, I didn't have to work the next day, and Michigan Zydeco was a favorite of mine, playing a mix of rock and bluegrass, and any night on the pier meant clams and crab and ice cold beer.

As I drove up to the house, the Suburban was there. Wednesday was Craig's day off, and he usually stayed around the house. I walked in, yelling hello.

My dogs, now that the girls were no longer a novelty, had gone back to their old habits, and were actually glad to see me again when I came through the door. I heard voices, and saw Craig outside, throwing a Frisbee to the twins. I walked out to them.

Maddie dropped the Frisbee and ran up to me, Larissa right behind.

"We went across the Bay Bridge."

"It was really cool."

"No, it was scary."

"Amanda wanted to go to the mall."

"Daddy bought her another phone."

"*We* can't have one till we're ten."

"So we had to come home right away so Amanda could do stuff."

"Keesha's here and sleeping over."

I crouched down and gave them both a hug. "What an exciting day. Did you eat?"

"Yes, there's pizza left over."

"I hate pepperoni and had to pick it all off."

I narrowed my eyes. "Maddie, last week you said pepperoni was your best food ever."

She made a face. "Not *this* pepperoni."

I stood up and looked at Craig. "Sounds like a good day?"

He nodded. "Yes, it was. And I'm not even exhausted." He looked well rested and happy, dressed in khaki shorts and a button down shirt, the sleeves rolled up.

"So, you want to go out to the pier tonight?" I didn't have a conscious thought to ask him. The words just fell out of my mouth. "It's Karen's birthday, there's a great band, and you can spend some play time with grown-ups."

He looked a little surprised, and I guess I couldn't blame him. "I don't want to leave the girls," he said.

"Stella told me that Keesha babysat her nieces. She's practically a professional. If she's sleeping over, I bet she and Amanda can handle these two with no problem."

"We're not a problem."

"We'll be good, Daddy."

"Don't you want to go to the birthday party?"

He was looking at me steadily, eyes expressionless, then suddenly smiled. "Sure. Why not? And I'll drive, so you can really celebrate with your friends."

"Well, now, thank you for that. I need to change." I practically danced all the way back to the house, but once I shut my bedroom door, I started kicking myself right in my own butt. What was I feeling so happy about? It's not like this was a date. Every woman on the pier would be all over him to dance, he'd probably never even talk to me...I hadn't felt such frustration since I asked Jimmy Rinaldi to the eighth grade dance and he'd said yes, then spent all night making out with Julie Blair.

That didn't stop me from digging out a dark green slip dress that came just to my knees, and curling my hair, letting it fall down my back in loose tendrils. I put in some dangly earrings and even managed a bit of lipstick and mascara. I looked critically in the mirror. Not too bad.

Then I shook my head. Good Lord, who was I kidding? We'd been living in the same house for months now. If he'd wanted me, he'd had plenty of chances to make a move. Obviously, he didn't find me desirable. Or, if he did, he was still too conscious of the fact that I'd spent five years—and then some—sleeping with his father, and my feeling was that was something he couldn't get past. Maybe I couldn't either. Did I really think being in a pretty dress and dancing under the stars would make him see me any differently?

On the off chance it would, I put on more mascara. Then I slipped on strappy sandals that wouldn't fall off my feet if I was dancing and went back to the living room.

Amanda and Keesha were on the couch, heads together, a bowl of Cheetos on Amanda's lap.

Amanda held up her phone, grinning excitedly. "Look, I have a new phone! It's so much cooler than my old one, and Keesha knows all the really good apps."

Keesha smiled modestly. "You taking Mr. Ferris to the pier?" she asked.

I nodded.

Keesha looked me up and down. "Well, you're looking pretty good. Have a nice time."

"Ah, thank you." At least I had *someone's* approval.

Amanda smiled. "I hope you and Daddy have a good time," she said. "I think you look really pretty too. Doesn't she Daddy?"

Craig, walking down the hall from his room, stopped short and stared at me.

"Doesn't she, Daddy?" Amanda repeated. "Doesn't Jenna look pretty?"

He nodded, his eyes never leaving my face, and I felt my cheeks start to get warm.

"I'll meet you in the car," I said, and practically ran out of the house.

I sat in the front seat of the Suburban, my brain racing. He was probably shocked to see me in something other than scrubs or jean shorts and a T-shirt. He probably forgot I had real hair. He'd never seen me in earrings. Maybe he was stunned by all the freckles. Maybe he was reminded that I really didn't have any boobs. There were million reasons for that stare, and most of them not all that great.

He got in beside me, turned on the ignition, and pulled out without a word. We were halfway to the highway before he spoke. "So, a good band?"

I nodded. "Yes. Michigan Zydeco. They play here a lot during the season. Fun music. It's not everyday you see a band where someone is playing a Jews Harp."

He chuckled. "True that. And it's Karen's birthday?"

"Yes, so all my crazy friends will be there. I know you've met them, but here's your chance to see us all at our finest."

"I like your friends. Will that woman who bought the house on Main, Terri's friend, will she be there?"

I felt my heart drop to my knees, but kept smiling. "Chris Polittano? I'm sure Terri will bring her along."

"She's really taking a leap, isn't she? Moving to a new place. It's brave, don't you think?"

"Yes," I said, my heart sinking. He thought she was *brave*? After that he would start thinking she was fearless and fascinating, then smart and sexy, and before you knew it they'd be having wild sex in the little house on Main Street.

We reached the highway. "Which way?"

"Left." I stared at my hands, then fiddled with the zipper of my purse. It was a tiny, beaded thing with a silky shoulder strap that fit my phone, one credit card and a small wad of cash.

"Is there food?"

"What." I'd been imagining a scenario where Chris and Craig danced the night away while I sat in a heap on the ladies room floor, crying. "Food where?"

"At the pier. I only had one slice of pizza."

"Oh, yes. Steamed clams, raw oysters, cracked crab...and their corn? Fresh picked, drenched in butter. And homemade biscuits. Oh, and po' Boys. The po' Boys are amazing."

He chuckled. "I love to hear you talk about food. You just... enjoy it so much."

"Other people's food, yes. You've seen me try to cook."

He was grinning now. "Yes, I certainly have. But you're very good at *growing* food."

I laughed. "Yes, I am."

"And you're also very good at *catching* food."

"Fish and crab. Again, very true. I just need someone to do the actual cooking. Right here, then another quick right."

He turned. "Well, the cooking is what I do best. That's why we're such a good team."`

I stared ahead, watching the familiar road. Yes, we had become a team, managing meals, trading chores, watching the girls. We were, I realized with a sudden shock, something of a family.

We came up to the entrance. "Here it is. Follow the drive to the end and find a place to park. We need to walk the rest of the way."

He pulled into an empty space, turned off the ignition, and smiled at me. "Ready?"

"You bet."

We got out and walked past the marina all the way to the end of the pier, and all I could think about was how he thought Chris was brave, and I was good at collecting food.

So much for my green dress and dangling earrings. This was *not* going the way I'd hoped.

Chapter Nine

They'd already grabbed a long table, and Karen stood and waved at me.

"Here we are! Craig, wow, hi! Thanks for coming!" She hugged me first, then Craig. "What's the deal? I never see you outside of Sam's."

He grabbed a stool. There were no chairs or benches at the pier, just short stools that could be easily moved from one table to the next. "Special occasion," he said. "It's not every day you have birthday. How could I resist?"

Karen's mouth dropped open in surprise. So did mine. Since when was he charming with relative strangers? Working the restaurant and bar had obviously loosened him up.

He waved across the table where Terri and Chris were diligently picking at a plate of crab. Was *that* the reason he was suddenly so talkative? "Ladies. How's the house coming along?"

Chris looked up and made a face. "I hate the smells. Everything smells. Fresh-cut lumber, drywall goop, heavy-duty wood glue, that stuff they use when they're soldering pipes...this experience has introduced me to an entirely new range of bad smells that I never knew existed."

Terri leaned toward Craig. "I love the smell of fresh-cut lumber."

He grinned. "Me too. What are you eating? It looks delicious."

Karen waved. "No table service here. Just go up to the counter and order."

Craig turned to me. "Come with? I have a feeling I'm going to need a pro."

"Sure." I was so happy at that moment. The lights strung around the pier were lit, I could hear the tree frogs and crickets, and I was surrounded by my friends. Soon, the music would start, and we'd all be up by the band, dancing, and Craig was with me. He was acting as relaxed and funny here in public as he was with me, and I felt almost proud of him. Two months ago he would have just sat there, nodding and saying polite things.

Then it struck me. Two months ago he was a total stranger, bringing his beloved daughters to an unknown town, looking for a place to catch his breath and maybe find some peace. He had no idea what he was walking into, and it could very well have ended badly. Now, he wasn't a stranger. He was a member of the community. He had a place in Cape Edwards, and so did his children. He could let his guard down and finally be himself. I felt a little rush of shame for thinking so badly of him those first weeks, because now I knew that he was, in fact, quite wonderful.

Would he dance with me? I'd seen him with Amanda when they sang together and knew he had rhythm and grace. Yes, I'd get him on the dance floor. At least once. Unless, of course, he spent all his time with Chris the Brave, Chris the Fascinating, Chris the...

At the counter, Wayne Harris gave me a wave. "Hey, Red, what can I get you?"

Craig looked down, where the menu was flattened and taped over onto the linoleum counter. "Well?"

"A beer and what? Seltzer? Two crab platters, extra butter, and a plate of steamers. Extra bread. Oh, and biscuits." I dug into my purse, but Craig put his hand on mine.

"This one's on me," he said.

I pulled my hand out from under his as quickly as I could, because I swear, my flesh was starting to smoke. "Thanks."

Wayne handed Craig his change and the receipt. "When your number comes up on the board, it's ready," he explained to Craig. "Here are your drinks."

We shouldered our way back to the table. I could feel him behind me, and it was all I could do to stop short, turn around and wrap my arms and legs around him, just to see what would happen.

Stella was sitting with Marie at the other end of the table with a striking woman with soft black skin and dreadlocks down her back. This, I thought, must be the new doctor in town. I scrambled around until I was crouching beside her.

Stella was beaming. "Jenna, this is Dara French. Dara, Jenna Ferris. The one I told you about?"

She flashed a smile, her teeth very white against her lips. "Pleased to meet you."

"Me too, I think. What exactly has Stella been telling you?"

She turned her head and looked down to the end of the table where Craig was listening, very intently, to something Terri was saying. Chris, I noticed, was watching his face, and he glanced briefly at her and smiled. Well...poop.

"That's some story you got going on," Dara said.

I sighed. "Yes, it is. And not even Stella knows the half of it. How's the house?"

Dara's face lit up. "Oh, it's gorgeous! Those two boys did such a good job! Now that I'm getting to know some people, I'm going to try to throw a little open house, maybe in the fall."

"You could probably sell tickets," I told her. "People have watched the Booker place go slowly downhill for years, and I bet lots of people are dying to see what it looks like."

She looked thoughtful. "Really?" She looked at Stella. "We need a fundraiser for the MedCenter. Do you all have a Christmas House Tour?"

Stella shook her head.

"I've been trying to put something like that together for years," Marie said.

Stella grinned at Dara "We might be able to put one together."

I bowed my head. "Well, my work here is done. Talk to you later."

I hurried back to my end of the table just as the music started, and I felt myself start to smile. I glanced up at the starry sky, then around the table. I had made a good life here, and as I looked at the laughing faces of my friends, I knew I would always be able to find some measure of happiness with these people.

I was feeling a positively benevolent glow when Olivia Kopechnie, dressed in a barely there tank top and flowing skirt, materialized out of nowhere and grabbed Craig's hand, and pulled him up and out toward the dance floor.

I watched and shook my head. Here I'd been waiting for him to make a move on Chris, or possibly, the other way around, and there was Olivia. It figured that she'd be the first to swoop in. I had no idea he'd be that easy. Then I got a tap on my shoulder, Kenny Malcom was smiling down at me.

"Looks like your date bailed."

I shook my head. "Not my date. Where's your wife, Kenny? Y'all fighting again?"

His smile widened. "She moved out. I'm whatcha call a free agent."

I narrowed my eyes at him. I had been interested in him a long time ago and knew of at least one area where we fit together pretty well. And I really needed something —or someone—to take my mind off of Craig Ferris. "Let's dance."

Olivia was showing Craig how to flatfoot. Flatfooting was dancing, similar to clogging, but without the high stepping knees and loud stomping. You danced by yourself, arms dangling, feet moving, and it was the kind of dance that anyone could learn quickly to become part of the crowd. Michigan Zydeco knew their audience, and always played plenty of country rock and bluegrass, just the right songs for flatfooting. Craig, I saw, was a fast learner.

Olivia probably didn't need to be standing practically on top of him, but she was so darn close if she got any closer she'd be on his other side.

Kenny was trying to get grabby but I kept dancing away. I looped arms a few times with Carl, who worked with Terri at the post office, and did a bit of flatfooting of my own with some guy, obviously a tourist, who kept trying to yell in my ear that I should go back to his boat. I finally noticed that our number was flashing up above the counter, weaved my way through the crowd, tugged on Craig's arm and pointed. He shrugged at Olivia and followed me, picked up our food, and headed back to the table.

Olivia was ready there, sitting on the stool right next to Craigs. In other words, mine.

The music stopped so I didn't have to yell. "I can't eat standing up, Olivia." She shot daggers at me, smiled sweetly at Craig, and moved on.

The steamers were a no brainer, but getting the most out of a crab required a bit of finesse. When I served the crabs I'd caught off the dock, I already cracked and picked them when I set them on the table, so it took a few minutes to show Craig the right way of twisting the claw just right for maximum meat with minimum effort.

After two minutes, I had to stop watching him eat. Every time he licked the butter off his fingers, I wanted to climb on his lap and offer him something else to lick.

Terri kicked me under the table. *You okay?* She mouthed.

I nodded, and concentrated on my corn.

"So," he said in my ear as the music started back up, "that was your boyfriend you were dancing with?"

His breath was warm on the back of my neck, and I felt a jolt run all the way down to my toes. I jerked my head around. "Who, Kenny? Who said he was my boyfriend?" But I knew the answer. Olivia. "He's not. At all."

"Oh?"

"What did Olivia say?"

He actually looked embarrassed. "That you slept with him?"

"Once. Years ago, before he was married. And we were both drunk. It was a rather...spontaneous one-time situation."

He nodded thoughtfully. "I've had a few of those myself." He pushed away his paper plate, littered with broken shells and biscuit crumbs. "God, that was good." He looked at my equally empty plate. "Can I ask you a personal question?"

"Sure."

"How do you manage to eat as much food as you do and still stay in such great shape?"

He thought I was in great shape? Oh, why did he have to say those kinds of things?

"Good metabolism," I told him. "Although my mother turned into one of those round Russian dolls when she hit sixty-five, so I'm on borrowed time."

He gathered up his plate and mine, as well as the rest of the assorted debris, and carried it to the large metal garbage can by the fence. On the way over, Olivia, with the precision of a top-flight guided missile, grabbed him again.

I think I would have been okay. I probably would have made it through the evening if Karen hadn't opened her birthday present from Marie, a bottle of Don Patron. With the salt and lemons all ready on the table, I was pretty much a goner. There's a country song about how tequila makes some girl's clothes come off. That might not have been exactly true for me, but shots had a tendency to loosen me up way more than was usually safe, and after my third shot I stormed onto the dance floor and butted right in between Craig and Olivia.

"Hey," she sputtered.

"He's my ride," I told her sweetly, and put my arms right around his neck and pulled him toward the edge of the crowd.

The song was coming to an end, and I was expecting another bluegrass tune, or maybe a bit of Charlie Daniels, but the lead singer leaned into the mike.

"Let's slow this one down."

And there I was, my arms around Craig Ferris, the lead singer crooning "Blue Bayou".

His hands went to my hips and in the faint light I could see his eyes twinkle. "Thanks. I was afraid she was going to eat me alive, right there in front of everyone."

I threw back my head and laughed out loud. "Seriously? What, you couldn't just pretend to go to the bathroom?"

"I'm not so good at putting off women," he said. The silence immediately became awkward. He hadn't had too much of a problem putting *me* off.

I was trying to keep as much air between us as I could, but he had a pretty good grip on my hips, and wasn't letting me go. I relaxed against him, and I felt the heat pouring off of him like honey melting in the summer sun. "Olivia has a bit of a reputation," I told him. "Usually, she finds plenty of entertainment during the season, but in the winter, when the picking are a bit slimmer, she gets downright dangerous."

"I'll have to remember that." His hand shifted a little lower to the curve of my hip.

I lifted my chin. "Does that mean you'll be here over the winter?"

The pier stuck right out into the inlet that came in from the bay, and there was a cool breeze off the water, but all I felt was heat. I moved my hands from around his neck on to his shoulders, and could feel the subtle play of his muscles as he moved. If I looked straight ahead, I could see directly into the cleft in his chin, so I had to look up into his eyes. He was looking down at me, his eyes still twinkling.

"The girls really like it here," he said. "Amanda has a friend. The twins have fifty friends. And it seems I've made one or two myself."

"Yes, you have. I bet Olivia would do practically anything for you."

He chuckled. "That's really not the kind of friendship I'm looking for."

"What, hot sex with a curvy blond isn't your thing?"

He shook his head very slowly. "No, actually. It's not my thing at all." His hands moved again, just enough that there was now not enough room between our bodies for a caterpillar to crawl through.

I laid my head against his chest and melted into him. His arms tightened. Were we even moving anymore? I think so, in slow circles. I could hear the drumming of his heart and felt his breath in my hair, and in that moment, I felt like I could have stayed there forever.

Then the music changed, and the drummer hit the cymbals, and we practically flew apart, the magic broken.

But it had been there. I felt it, and knew that he had too.

Thank God he had decided to drive, because all I was good for on the way home was hanging my head out the window and singing at the top of my lungs.

It was late. Very late. I knew that he'd texted Amanda on her new phone, and she'd told him that everything and everyone was fine, so he laughed and said, sure, I could have another shot. And then a beer, and then another, and then we danced again, flat footing to Fox on the Run, and Foggy Mountain Breakdown, and The Devil Went Down to Georgia. The band bowed its way out and we were still there, until Wayne had to come out and tell Karen that her birthday was over.

Terri had her golf cart with her, and I knew it was a five-minute drive back to her condo. Stella and Dara had left early, as did Marie, and Terri and Chris talked Karen into going home with them. Olivia had left, but there was another table besides ours that stayed, laughing and talking too far into the night.

Nights without a moon on the Eastern Shore were dark. No one had thought too much about streetlights, and even the state road was pitch black. Luckily, there were always lights on in the church, and Craig didn't need me to tell him where to turn. Not that I was capable of telling him. As we turned off the highway, I was dangling both of my arms out the window and singing, "Do not forsake me, oh, my darling."

When we made the turn toward the house, I pulled myself back into the Suburban and put my finger to my lips.

"Shhh. We can't wake up the girls."

He chuckled. "No, we can't. But the dogs might."

I waved both hands at him. "No. They only bark at strangers in the nighttime. Or squirrels. But squirrels are usually asleep. The raccoons are awake. And listen? Can you hear them?"

He stopped the car and turned off the ignition. We heard the owls.

I got out of the car and and looked out at the Bay. I could barely see the whitecaps as the water hit the shore, and the sky was so dark every star sparkled. As always, it drew me, and I ran to the water's edge.

There was a stand of white pine close to the bay, and I knew that's where the owls nested. I stood still, eyes closed, and felt the breeze off the water and heard the lapping of the waves against the rocks, the soft hoot of the owls. Eyes still closed, I started spinning, twirling like I hadn't done since I was a little girl, opening my eyes suddenly to see the flash of starlight, the glistening of the bay, and Craig's face. I stopped and stumbled right into his arms, and I reached up and kissed him.

There were words. I knew there were words, I heard them, but louder than anything was the rushing of blood in my ears, and the pounding of my heart. There was no one to interrupt us now, out under the stars, no one to see or hear us but the night birds watching from above. He pulled my dress up and over my head in one quick, fluid motion, and his hands and his mouth were everywhere as we tumbled to the tall, damp grass. My fingers felt too thick and slow as I tugged at the buttons of his shirt, then his zipper. I eased onto him slowly, and he let out a low groan, and then we began to move, with none of the fumbling or awkwardness of two people who had never been together before. We fit perfectly, and moved as one, until we both cried out in the starlight.

I lay on top of him until my breathing slowed, and I shifted away from him, but he caught me, and pulled me back so that he could kiss me again very gently this time, on the lips.

"Do you know how long I've been wanting to do this?" he whispered.

"What were you waiting for?" I asked.

"For you to forgive me for being such a damn fool."

I kissed him against the side of his mouth. "Next time," I said, "just ask."

I stood and looked around, picked up my dress and panties off the ground, and held them against me. My heart was ready to explode. Our coming together had not just been about flesh meeting flesh. Something had been broken through, a barrier that I'd been running against for weeks had suddenly opened for me. Craig Ferris was all I wanted now. Everything I'd been dreaming about was now real, and a feeling of joy like I'd never known before flooded through me.

"Let's go to bed," I said. He followed me inside, through the back door and into my room, where I chased the dogs out and threw my clothes in the corner, followed by his. I lit a single candle and we lay down on the bed, facing each other, on top of the sheet, the breeze from the Bay cooling our bodies.

We talked about everything. We compared childhoods. We talked about high school. We already knew so much about each other, but I felt like I could spend the rest of my life listening to him and learning more. Sometime in the dead of night, we made love again, starting slower, taking our time.

And when I woke in the morning, the sun was streaming in and my dogs were all back in bed with me, and he was gone.

I could hear the voices drifting down the hallway, and felt a rush of relief. They were eating breakfast. Of course. He had to get up and make breakfast and drive the girls to the playground. That feeling of joy rushed through me again. Could I possibly spend the rest of my life waking up like this? Knowing that Craig and I were together? Hearing him in the kitchen, making breakfast for a family that was now mine? I pulled on a tank top and some shorts and padded to the kitchen.

He was at the stove, wearing baggy gym shorts and a T-shirt. He looked up when I entered and gave me a shy, sweet smile. "Good morning, sleepyhead. Pancakes?"

Keesha looked at me critically. "You sure look like *you* had a good time."

I poured some coffee and sat beside her. "How old are you again?"

She giggled and looked at Amanda as though to say *what's with this crazy woman?*

Maddie had the answer. "Keesha is thirteen, just like Amanda."

"Except Amanda's birthday is in October, and Keesha's is in April."

"Keesha's older."

"Was it a fun party?"

"Did you bring us cake?"

"How old was your friend?"

"When is *your* birthday?"

My head was surprisingly clear, no trace of a hangover. "December first. Karen is fifty-one. There was no cake. And the party was pretty terrific."

Craig put a plate of steaming pancakes in front of me. His eyes were dancing and his mouth twitched. "Yes, I especially liked the after party." He clapped his hands together. "We leave in five minutes, everyone. Plates in the sink and brush your teeth."

There was a rush to the sink, then we were alone.

"So, listen." He stopped.

I poured plenty of syrup on the pancakes, then looked up, waiting.

"Last night was...wonderful."

I smiled so wide my cheeks hurt. "Yeah, it was."

"I think that maybe you and I should talk about it a little more."

"Or we could not so much talk as just try to repeat the experience."

He chuckled. "Yes, we could certainly do that." His smile vanished. "It's...you were really drunk last night."

I put down my knife and fork. "Not that drunk. And maybe the first time, but..." I smiled. "Not the second time."

His mouth twitched. "True that. I just want to make sure."

I felt a little twist in my gut. "Make sure about what?"

He ran his hand through his hair, and tugged at the ends. "That first time you kissed me, up in Dad's place, I got the feeling that it wasn't all about me."

This was not necessarily the conversation I wanted to have first thing in the morning after a night of pretty spectacular sex. "I will admit," I said slowly, "there were a lot of emotions involved that day."

He looked at me, his eyes steady. "You were thinking about my father."

I pushed my plate away. "You really want to talk about this *now*?" I heard the front door open, and Maddie calling his name. "Seriously?"

"I will not," he said slowly, "be a substitute." He turned abruptly and left, and seconds later, I heard the front door slam.

I stared at my pancakes, then the empty space where Craig had just stood. Substitute? After what happened between us, he really thought I was using him as a Sam replacement? Did he not hear the things I said to him? Did he not understand that it was *him* I wanted, not the ghost of husbands past?

I got up, leaving my breakfast untouched, and went in to change into some real clothes.

This conversation was not over. Not by a long shot.

He was at the restaurant, in the small office behind the kitchen.

The desk was covered with invoices, and he was frowning at his computer. I banged the door shut behind me and stood, hands on hips, glaring down at him.

"Did you not hear a word I said last night?" I hissed. "Did you really imagine, even for a second, that I thought you were *Sam*?"

He sat back in his chair and folded his hands, very calmly, in his lap. "When we were up in Dad's apartment and you kissed me, you were thinking about my father. You admitted it."

He had to play his Ace card right away? Who *did* that? "Yes, I admitted that, Craig. And I'll put this out here right now, from the minute I saw you I wanted, that is, there was a very serious physical attraction." Wait. Was I helping my case here? "But the truth is, even if I'd never seen Sam Ferris before in my life, I still would have felt the same because from a purely personal perspective I would have wanted to jump your bones anyway. I think you're really hot."

He nodded his head in short, abrupt jerks. "I'm hot? That's it? Last night was about me being your idea of a good time?"

"No. Yes. It *was* about a good time. But—"

"You know, that's what your friend Olivia was all about, and I turned her down flat."

"First of all, she is not my friend. And good for you for turning her down, because you might have caught something. But—"

"I didn't use a condom last night, which was my mistake. Do I have to worry about catching something from you? Because apparently, Olivia isn't the only woman around here who has a reputation for sleeping around."

That stopped me cold. I literally had to clench my fists and rein back all the things that rushed into my brain. *Think, Jenna, think before you speak. Think before you speak.*

I'd done a lot of things I wasn't proud of, slept with men I should have left alone, and generally spent a few years as a basic screw-up. I'd forgiven myself for those actions and was not about to start feeling guilty all over again. And no one, not even Craig

Ferris, was going to make me feel bad about myself for things done in the past.

"Is it true that you slept with him even after the divorce?" His voice was still calm, but looking into his eyes I could see the anger slowly coming to the surface.

"Olivia really gave you an earful," I managed.

"Not just Olivia."

I unclenched my fists and took a couple of deep, cleansing breaths. How could he look like that, so calm, while my whole world was starting to crumble? "All I really want you to know is that last night, I wanted you, Craig Ferris. Not Sam, not just any hot guy, *you*." I waited for him to understand, to realize what I was saying, what I was feeling, but the mask was still there. This was the moment, I realized. I was going to have to put myself out there, one hundred percent, or he was going to slip away. I took a deep breath. "Because I think I'm in love with you."

"And how can you tell, Jenna? How do you know you're just not still in love with Sam? You said yourself he ruined you for other men, and I know I'm not at all like him. He was larger than life, my father, and I am only a very regular guy who happens to look just like him."

I saw them falling, all those pretty castles in the air I had built just an hour before. I'd spent weeks pining after this man, trying to show him how I felt, not crowding him, trying to build a relationship with him based on friendship and trust. Obviously, I failed miserably.

"None of this seemed to bother you last night, Craig." The words spilled out before I could stop them, and I clench my fists again. *Stupid, stupid stupid...*

"You're not the only one who likes a good time."

And there it was. "So much for your righteous anger, Craig. Obviously, it doesn't matter to you how many men *I* slept with, or who I thought I was screwing last night, because as far as you're concerned, you got laid. Period. And that's all that really mattered, right?" The top of my head was coming off. I was so angry in that moment I wanted to scream, throw something, hit something...

His mouth twisted, and for just a second, I thought he was going to tell me I was wrong, that last night had meant something to him as well, something real and important.

"True that."

I whirled and jerked the door open, then slammed it behind me. I stormed past Glory, standing open mouthed. I burst out onto the sidewalk, knocking into a mom and her kids on the way to the beach, sending plastic pails flying. I mumbled an apology and scrambled to retrieve the assorted beach toys scattered on the cement. I was crying, hot and angry tears, and people may have been staring, but I didn't care. I didn't care about anything.

I got to the Jeep and called the hospital, getting through to the HR department. I had three weeks vacation, I explained, and I wanted to take it all, as soon as possible.

There were stammers and stalls. After all, summer was the busiest time in the ER. Usually, no vacation time was granted between the Fourth of July and Labor Day. Maybe a few days, but...

I clicked off the phone and leaned forward, my forehead against the steering wheel, and squeezed my eyes closed, my jaw clenched so tight I thought my teeth would crack.

I was stuck here, with Craig, after I told him I thought I was in love with him, and he didn't say it back. He acted like he didn't even *care* that I'd said it. That was enough. I was done.

I called Ellis Summer and told him I wanted the property to be divided into two separate lots, one in my name, and one in Craig's. Then I asked him to start the paperwork for me to buy out Craig's half of the house.

The sooner he was out of my life, the better.

Chapter Ten

You'd think that it would be hard to avoid a person living in the same house as you, but, with a little work, it was surprisingly easy. I managed to go two whole weeks and was only in the same room with him at the same time twice.

He was putting in a very concerted effort as well. I don't know what he said to his daughters. I still spent Thursdays with them. I picked them up from the playground, and we spent the day at the house. Maddie finally caught a rockfish, and I cleaned it for her before she presented it to her father to cook for dinner. The girls didn't ask why I wasn't eating with them. They nodded at my excuses to be somewhere else Sunday afternoons. They didn't even question my not sitting with them at church.

I was so unhappy I wanted to crawl under my dock and drown.

I knew when Ellis presented him with my proposal to sell him half the property because he actually knocked on my bedroom door to talk to me.

"This is a good plan, about dividing the land. I'll sign the papers," he said stiffly.

I crossed my arms across my chest. "Fine."

"But you can't buy me out yet. I need a place to live."

"How's the job hunt?"

He finally met my eyes. "I have a third interview. The company is down in Richmond. I should know by the end of the month if we'll be moving."

"Perfect. Will you sell to Glory?"

"If she can get financing."

"Good."

"Yes. Good." He walked back down the hall, and I crept back into my bed, hugging Bit to my broken heart.

I'd also managed to stay away from my friends, which was much harder. I didn't want to explain to them, not yet anyway, because it still felt too raw. Yes, guys, we danced at the pier, and I spun around in the starlight, and then we made love in the grass, and then again in my bed, and then we had a huge fight and now he hates me. End of story.

I just couldn't.

But I'd driven down Main Street, and saw the progress of Chris Polittano's new house. Curiosity got the best of me, and I pulled in the back alley to take a look.

The yard had been emptied of debris and had been scraped down to bare dirt, and there were piles of lumber and what looked to be boxed kitchen cabinets carefully pushed against the new siding, under a blue tarp to protect them from the weather. The old back porch was gone, the former doorway replaced by a double-hung window, and there was obviously a lot of activity inside. I walked around to the side, through the new door and took a few steps in.

Terri was standing there and she was wearing a hard hat. I had to try very hard not to laugh. I failed.

"Where have you been?" she yelped. "Did you have the plague?"

"Why aren't you at work?" I grumbled. If I had known she'd be there, I would not have stopped.

"I promised Chris I'd spend my vacation working, and here I

am." She leaned in and searched my face intently. "What happened? It's Craig, right? Oh, Jenna, what did you do?"

"We had a night of ecstasy, and then we stopped talking to each other."

"Oh, Jenna," she sighed.

I looked around. There was a floor, and walls, and even sheetrock. I could see the kitchen roughed in, and from the back of the house, the whirring of power tools.

She pulled off her hat and yelled toward the back of the house. "Steve, I'm on the porch for a sec."

I followed her out. The porch floor had also been replaced, as well as the rotten railing. We sat on the new front steps.

"Tell me," she said. "The ecstasy part first."

"It was after the night at the pier. I was drunk, but not that drunk, and I pretty much attacked him in my back yard, and then we went into the house and he attacked me, and then we had a giant fight and we've been avoiding each other ever since."

"Jenna, honey, you live in the same house."

"Yes, and that makes things difficult, but not impossible. I'm taking a few days vacation myself, going up to Boston to visit my cousin, Clare. He's got a third interview somewhere, so maybe by the time I get back he'll have accepted a job and will move the hell out of my house."

"Oh, Jenna, but what about Amanda? You know, I've seen her, and she looks so much happier, and you did that."

I felt tears. "Not me," I snapped. "She's got a best friend now. I had nothing to do with anything."

"Of course you did," Terri said. "And you love that little girl. And the twins. Jenna, what are you going to do?"

"I don't know," I moaned. "And I'm going to miss them, and I love him, Terri, and he thinks I only slept with him because he was so much like Sam, and maybe that would have been true before, but...he's so great, he really is, and he thinks I'm a, a, oh..." I wiped the tears from my face with both hands and sniffed. "He hates me."

"I doubt that. You're really a great person, too, Jenna. Any fool can see that."

"Well, obviously there's one fool who can't." I sniffed some more and watched as a car full of teen boys sped down Main Street. "Have any drunks puked on your brand new walkway yet?" I asked.

"No, not yet. But the summer isn't over."

I nudged her with my knee. "And Steve McCann?"

She shut her eyes and tightened her lips. "He asked Chris out, but she said no."

"Oh? Well, that's...a good thing?"

"Yes. Because she has developed a very strong crush on Mike."

I choked, trying not to laugh. "Are you kidding?"

She opened her eyes. "You cannot make this stuff up."

"Don't the brothers talk to each other? I mean, isn't at least one of them keeping score here?"

"Apparently not."

"Men."

"I *know!*"

"What are you going to do?"

She blew out noisily. "Well, I was thinking about accidentally taking all my clothes off one afternoon, but Steve is never here alone, and it could get awkward."

"True."

"Or I could pretend to faint and force a little mouth-to-mouth action, but with my luck the plumber would get to me first, and that would be nasty."

I stopped trying to not laugh and let loose. "Terri, you are too much."

"Well, what else can I do?" she asked.

"Did you ask him to meet you for dinner some night to discuss the work?"

She frowned. She sat straighter and tilted her head, obviously thinking very hard. "That's a good idea."

"You think?"

"That might actually work. I'd have to figure out how to keep Chris out of the conversation. After all, it's her house."

"Yes, but you are the force behind this project."

"Yes. I am."

"You are, how can we say this...the brains behind the operation."

"No, not really. I mean, Chris is *really* smart. But Steve might not know that."

"Absolutely."

"What are *you* going to do?"

My shoulders slumped. "Terri, I am at a loss. I have no idea what I can do or say to make him believe me, especially since he refuses to be alone in a room with me."

"Write him a letter?"

I shot her a look. "Seriously?"

"I want to help."

"I know."

She laid her head on my shoulder. "We really miss you at breakfast."

"I know. I'll be back. I miss you guys, too." I looked back at the house. "The house looks good."

She nodded. "Yes, it does. Chris is really happy."

"Where is she?"

"Went back to Rehoboth. Tying up loose ends."

"Ah. So you won't have to try to get her out of the way?"

It took her a second, then her eyes widened. "That's right! Oh, my gosh. But where would we go? Anywhere around here and the rumor mill would run into overtime."

I stood up. "The rumor mill is always running into overtime. Olivia filled Craig's head with all sorts of goodies."

She looked uncomfortable. "Yes. Olivia has been busy."

I turned to her. "What has she been saying?"

"How much of a disgrace it is for you to be chasing after your stepson. Like he was a young thing you'd help raise from the cradle, and now..."

I exhaled loudly. "Well, she certainly picked up on a fairly hot topic."

She stood next to me. "But, Jenna, it's not like that, not at all, and we all know it. Olivia always tries to spoil the well if she can't be the one drinking from it."

"Yes, but still..." I shrugged. "It doesn't matter anyway. It's all over."

"I'm so sorry, sweetie. And thanks, Jenna. Really. For stopping by, and for all the good advice."

I gave her a quick hug. "Sure thing. Keep me in the loop."

"There's a loop?"

I nodded. "Always." I walked back to the Jeep and headed home.

Boston was wonderful. I stayed with my cousin and her husband for five days, and played tourist with her and her three kids. One night we did the Patriots Path Pub Crawl, stopping and drinking in the very same pubs that Samuel Adams and his ilk frequented while planning a revolution. We also saw Plimouth Plantation, and I marveled how any group of people could be so successful under such adverse conditions. I almost felt better about my own situation. Sure, I was miserable, but at least I didn't have to chop my own wood and grind dried corn to keep from starving to death.

Craig had promised to take care of the dogs, Dave took goat duty, and Amanda said she would look after the garden. I came home late that weekend, missed church, and spent a Sunday afternoon gathering tomatoes and zucchini. I had enough for a small army.

My being away had not eased the tension between Craig and I. When I came home from my shift, I changed quickly, then went right back out. There was a note on the counter late Wednesday night when I came in that the girls were spending the afternoon with Keesha's father the next day, and that there was no need for me to get them from the playground.

That was why I was home the next morning, a hot, muggy and miserable morning, when a shiny new Cadillac pulled up in front of the house.

The dogs went crazy. I was in the garden, sweating and elbow deep in compost, and completely baffled. Who the hell was this? Did people really drive a Cadillac anymore outside of the movies?

I called to Chloe and Finn and walked over, scooping up Bit and looking at the car.

It had an Illinois plate.

The man who got out was short and stocky, with silver-gray hair and expensive sunglasses. In fact, everything he had on reeked of money, from the thick gold chain around his neck to his highly polished shoes. He looked out at the water first, then at the house, then at me.

"Nice place," he said. "Must be worth a pretty penny."

The woman who got out was much younger, her perfectly cut ash blond hair screamed money, as did her very chic sunglasses.

"Can I help you?" I asked.

"I'm looking for Craig Ferris," the man said. He held out a hand. "Robert Cordane."

I held up my hands, one caked with dirt, the other holding Bit, and shrugged apologetically. "Why?"

He smoothly put his hand into his pocket. "Actually, I'm looking for my granddaughters. I believe they're living here? With Craig?" I could only imagine what he thought of me, standing there with my messy bun and muddied Doc Martens. "And you, I suppose."

"How did you find the house?" I asked. I looked past him to the woman, who was coming around the car, tottering on very high heels.

"Googled it, what else? I must admit I was beginning to think the GPS was broken. Not much out here, is there?"

"How did you even know they were here?" I asked.

"Public records are, well, public. I looked up Ferris' will. I tried to get a judge to bring him back to Illinois, but..." He shrugged. "If Mohammad won't come to the mountain..."

The hate I felt for this man was sudden and completely unfounded, but very real. From his car to his gold chain and pinky ring, his smug attitude...was this the man who'd been trying to take the girls away from Craig?

"They aren't here," I said. I looked from him to her. He didn't even introduce his wife? What. A .Jerk.

"At all?" he asked. "Or at this moment?"

I pulled Bit closer to my chest and glared.

"I have the address of the bar, too," he said. "I'll look there next. Do the girls spend a lot of time with him there?"

His wife fluttered her hands. One of those. "That's not good for the children, I'm sure."

"It's fine for the children," I shot back. "They're close to the beach, they're close to their father, people look after them...it's fine. It's more than fine."

Robert took off his sunglasses and looked at me through narrowed eyes. "He's working at a bar," he said slowly. "The man is a drunk, and he's working at a *bar*."

I saw where this was going and was suddenly afraid. "He owns a restaurant, a very successful one, that happens to have a bar. And he goes to a meeting every week."

"Are you sleeping with him?" he asked, a dirty, smug twist on his lips.

"Not that's any of your business, but no."

"Of course it's our business," the woman said shrilly.

I jerked my chin at her. "And who are you?"

"Penny. I'm the girls' grandmother, and I have very real concerns about their well being, living all the way out here in the middle of nowhere, spending time in a *bar*."

"Yeah? Well, guess what? I'm also their grandmother, and I'm telling you they're happy and safe and getting along just fine. I don't know what you think you're going to do here, but I want you to leave. Now."

Robert let out a whoop of a laugh. "You're their *what?*"

"I was married to Sam. Sam was their grandfather. So that makes me their grandmother." I nodded toward Penny. "As much as *she* is, anyway."

Robert put his sunglasses back on. "We'll find him. Is it far?"

"Google it."

He took a step toward me. "Listen lady, we're going to find him, so you may as well tell us an easy way to get out of here. You don't want to become involved in this. This Podunk little place isn't going to be able to protect you if things start to go badly for you."

"Get off my property before I call the police and have you arrested for trespassing. This Podunk place doesn't think too highly of fat cats who think they can threaten folks in their own front yards."

Chloe moved to my side and began to growl, very softly. Robert glanced down at her, then opened the car door and got back in. Penny scurried around, got in her side, and the car started and took off in a rather impressive display of flying gravel.

What a pig. Not only was he a pompous ass, he didn't even open the car door for his wife.

I pulled my phone out of my pocket and called the bar.

"Charlie, It's Jenna. I need to talk to Craig."

I heard him put the phone down and came back seconds later. "Craig's busy."

I clenched my jaw and took a breath. "Tell him Robert Cordane just left."

It took less than ten seconds.

"What?"

I started to tremble. "Robert Cordane. He just left here in a big Caddy. His wife was with him. They wanted to know where you were, where they girls were."

"Did you tell him?"

"God, no!" Amanda had said Grandpa Rob wanted to take

them away. That was why they were here, to try to get his grand-daughters.

"How did they find us?" he whispered. I could hear the fear in his voice.

"He said he got the address from Sam's will. Do you think he'd just take them?"

He swore. "I don't think so, but I don't know how far he'd go."

"You mean, like, *kidnapping* them?" I said, my voice rising. I started to run toward the house.

He swore again. "He's rich. He's not used to not getting what he wants."

I grabbed my keys and headed back out to the Jeep. "I'll get them at the playground and drive them across the bridge. It doesn't matter what kind of money he has if he can't find them. They can stay at my mother's place until you find out what's going on."

There was complete silence. I got in the car and turned the ignition. "Craig?"

"You'd do that for me?"

I leaned forward and leaned against the steering wheel. "Do you really think I'd let anyone take those girls away?"

More silence, then, "Thank you, Jenna, and listen—"

"I'll listen later. After I get the girls across the Bay."

I got in the Jeep, my heart in my throat. I knew all along in the back of my mind that when Craig left, Amanda and the twins would go with him. I'd been trying to imagine what that would be like. They had all become a part of my life, and I knew I would miss them terribly. But the thought of Craig losing them was almost too much to think about.

I couldn't let that happen. I didn't even know what I could do to help, but I had to help him.

Because I loved him and couldn't bear him being hurt.

Amanda, when I told her, turned white. "He took Daddy to court," she whispered. "I was so afraid he would take us away." The fear was coming off her like a wave. "Is that why he's here?"

I hugged her. "Baby, I will not let *anyone* take you away. Got that? We just have to get you someplace else for a while. You up for that?"

She nodded, went back to the counselors, talked to Keesha, and minutes later we were all headed for the Chesapeake Bay Bridge.

"Why does your mommy want to meet us?"

"Where does your mommy live?"

"Is there a pool?"

"Will Daddy be there?"

"I'm hungry. Is there food?"

"We never had a sleepover before. We need our pajamas."

"When we get there," I told them, "we'll make a list of stuff you need, and I'll bring it to you, okay?"

Crossing the Bay Bridge in summer was never fun, and it seemed to take forever before we came to Mom's. Sharon was at work, but Mom had the situation under control. I hadn't told her much on the phone, but when we finally got there, she had premade baloney sandwiches, my childhood favorite, and lemonade for lunch. She'd even baked chocolate chip cookies.

Amanda had put on weight during the summer, and that thin, pinched look was gone from her face. But at lunch, she looked almost as she had the first day she'd arrived: sad and afraid. Watching her pick apart her sandwich made my heart twist. I wasn't going to let anyone hurt her. Not again.

The girls always had their bathing suits and towels in their packs for the playground, so it was an easy fix to get them down and in the pool. Mom, who rarely left the balcony, looked offended when I said I'd watch them.

"Jenna dear, they need things. You need to bring those things. I can certainly watch them. I can sit right here under the umbrella and make sure they don't drown. Go do what you need to do. And you could use a shower, dear. Imagine, trying to steal little girls in this day and age. Why, that Cordane person should be arrested for just thinking about it."

So I drove over the Bay Bridge again and went back home. I showered, changed, and packed up the list of indispensable items that Amanda and the twins compiled. It took two suitcases.

By the time I made it to Cape Edwards, it was dinnertime. I had to park illegally in the alley behind Main Street and snuck in the back door to Sam's on Main.

Craig was in the bar. Actually, he was behind the bar, mixing a drink with what looked like expert precision. I watched him for a minute, then pushed my way up to the bar.

"You've gotten good at that," I said.

He glanced up. "Yeah. I have. Give me a second."

I backed into a corner and waited. He came around, grabbed me by the arm, and we went through the storeroom and back into the alley.

"Tell me exactly," he said. I did, leaving out nothing, not even my mothers request that I shower. He stood, head bent, arms folded against his chest.

"Robert was here," he said when I was done. "He's got nothing. I called Chicago. Rob filed an appeal, but the judge struck it down. My lawyer told the judge I had relocated permanently, and the judge said if Robert wanted custody, he'd have to move down to Virginia to try again."

Relief flooded through me. "Then this is over?"

He shook his head. "Robert bought a place in Virginia Beach. A condo. It's not a permanent address, but it's good enough. He's going to take another shot."

"How much money does this guy *have?*"

He cracked a grim smile. "A boatload. Which was one of his arguments, that he could provide for the girls. He also probably thought he could use the bar against me, but that won't work either because I can start the job in Richmond September first."

I was very still. I could hear the traffic on Main Street, and the noise of the ice machine that stood right inside the door. "Oh?"

He didn't look at me. Instead, he focused on something directly over my right shoulder. "It's not ideal, but the money is outstanding and there are good schools in Richmond."

"There are good schools here," I said.

"Not really."

"Amanda is thriving here," I argued. I fought to keep my voice even. "And you have friends here. You even said, that night on the pier..."

He looked at me then, his eyes unreadable. "This was always the plan, Jenna."

"I know, but..." My voice broke. Damn him, anyway, him and his stupid job and his stupid daughters moving away. I didn't need this. I didn't need him. I was going to go to my mothers and bring his girls back and let him deal with this. Then I was going to find Kenny Malcolm and screw his brains out.

"I'll get the girls."

"Please, not yet."

"They're in Virginia Beach, Craig. That's where Robert is. What if he sees them? At least here we can stash them at Stella's. She has a huge house, I mean, she had six kids. Or Terri's. She's right down on Main, over the wine shop."

His mouth twitched. "That's convenient."

I rolled my eyes. "Right? I keep telling her to install a dumb waiter so she can just call and have something sent up."

He smiled, and the normalcy of it felt like balm on an open wound. Were we back? Two people just talking, joking, being friends?

He paused. "I think they should be okay back here. I mean, he wouldn't grab them forcibly. Now that we know that he's here and what he wants, we can be careful."

I nodded. He said *we*. "Whatever you think is best, Craig. But I think we need to wait until tomorrow. My mother is making lasagna for the girls, and Maddie was a little excited."

"I bet." He ran his hands through his hair. "I...I can't thank you enough."

"I don't want those little girls hurt," I said. "Or you."

Another pause. "I'll get over there tomorrow. Bring them home."

"Why don't I just camp over there myself and bring them home tomorrow? You'll have to feed the dogs."

"I can do that." He was staring over my shoulder again.

"Listen, Craig...you were behind the bar."

He frowned. "So?"

"You're okay with that?"

He sighed. "I already called Ted. He's my sponsor. I talked to him right after I got off the phone with you."

I nodded. "Good."

"And since I'm on my own tonight, I can find a meeting." He looked down at me at last. "Thank you. For being concerned."

I put my palm, very lightly, on his chest. "I'll see you tomorrow."

And all the ride over, and through dinner and watching Harry Potter, and sleeping with my sister while Amanda and the twins took the sleeper sofa, all I could think about was...he said 'we'.

"Your mom makes really good food. Why didn't she teach *you* to cook?"

"Is your sister older or younger than you?"

Amanda was still tense and withdrawn on the ride back. It was a crappy day, heavy rain falling and the traffic unbearable. Usually on Friday, I'd be going to my mother's. My brain was having a hard time breaking a five-year-old habit.

We slogged through the muddy road up to the house and I saw that the Suburban was there. The girls tumbled out and raced through the rain. Craig was at the door, arms wide, and he managed to get all three of them in one swoop. I followed, lugging the suitcases as they went into the house. They had me pack enough for a week's stay and managed to go through every item in just one night.

I closed the door, and he was right behind me.

"I got this," he said, taking the cases from my hands. He carried them effortlessly down the hallway, calling for the girls to unpack.

"But I have to say hello to Finn."

"Can we just put everything in the hamper?"

"My bathing suit was wet when I packed. Will that make a difference?"

I walked across the living room and gazed out at the water. It was so gray that the sky and the water blended together as a whole. The water was choppy. There had been warnings of the first hurricane of the season coming up the coast. The Eastern Shore was rarely bothered with a direct hit, but the unsettled ocean could make the bay choppy and rough. It had been hot and sticky outside, and the air conditioning caused a rim of condensation around the window.

"How about a cup of tea?" he said behind me. "It seems like a hot cup of tea day."

I turned. "Yes, it does. Thanks."

He broke open a package of Lorna Doones, and poured the hot water into my china teapot.

"That was my grandmother's," I told him. "I always used it for decoration. I don't think I ever made a pot of tea in it. I always used bags."

"Bags? Bah. Never. A scoop of loose tea per cup, let the boil go down so the temperature drops just a bit, pour the water over and let it steep."

"I forgot that everything in your life has a routine."

He carefully walked the steaming pot over to the table, then glanced up at me. "You make that sound like a bad thing."

"It's not. It's just not *my* thing."

"Yes. I noticed."

I took a cookie and bit, grateful for the quiet, the easy conversation. We were just two folks, having a cup of tea. No drama. No anger. No tension so thick you could slice it with a knife.

"Why did you do what you did yesterday? When Robert came? Why didn't you tell him where we were and be done with it?"

I stared at him. "Well, first of all, he was a pompous jerk, and he didn't even introduce his wife, so he was also a pompous *asshole*, and I didn't like him. That gold chain? Seriously? And he was smug. *And* he insinuated all sorts of things about you that I didn't like. Penny, by the way? A real bitch. Then he insulted my town, called it Podunk. When I told him to leave, he threatened me. Did you really think I'd let him get close to Amanda? Or the twins? No friggin' way." I ate another cookie in one bite. "I would have driven them back up to Boston to keep them away from him."

He started to laugh, first a chuckle, them a full-blown belly laugh. He pressed his palms to his eyes and shook his head. "Oh, Jenna, you are truly one of a kind." He dropped his hands. "I wish I had been here to see that."

I grinned. "Next time, I'll try to get video."

He poured us tea, and I had to admit, it was much better than a bag.

I dunked a cookie. "Is Ellis handling this for you?"

He shook his head as he blew on his tea to cool it. "Yes. He got me a name, someone who specializes in this sort of thing if it gets sticky, but he's taking charge. I'm having everything from my Chicago lawyer sent down." He took a sip, put the cup down, and took a breath. "Debbie was his only daughter, and he never believed she had any problems. He belittled me when I was drinking. I don't blame him. I was not a very good husband or father. But when Deb was killed and he found out that she'd been using painkillers, it triggered something. He went after me full bore. We'd been living in a house that he owned, that he'd bought for Deb, and after he lost the court hearing, he gave me three days to get out. I knew what he expected, that I wouldn't be able to find a new place to live, and he'd have another reason to go after his granddaughters." He shook his head. "They're all he has left of her. I get it. And I would have been happy to let him in their lives, but Rob was too selfish. He wanted them all for himself."

My tea was cool enough to drink. I took a few sips. "What was Deb like?"

He shrugged. "Spoiled. Very spoiled. And beautiful, and fun... God, she loved a good time. Smart, but not a whole lot of common sense, you know?"

"And you loved her like crazy, right?"

He nodded ruefully. "Oh, yeah. I would have done anything for her. And then two years ago she found some guy named Phil and she packed up all my stuff and changed the locks. I came home from work and couldn't get into my house. Her father's house. We just lived there." He shrugged. "I moved in with a buddy and then we went to war."

I drank more tea and began to break off tiny pieces of cookie, concentrating hard. As much as Sam had hurt me by leaving, he had never been cruel. We had never been at war. I knew what it felt like to have someone you know and love suddenly break your heart, but a betrayal like that was something I could not even imagine. Having gone through something like that once, it was no wonder he was so careful in guarding his heart.

When I lifted my eyes, he was looking puzzled.

"Are you planning to leave a trail of cookie crumbs somewhere?"

"What? Oh, no, I just don't know what to say."

"Well, there's a first."

I smiled. "Thank you for telling me."

"Yeah. Well..."

We sat in silence. Bit jumped on my lap and started sniffing at the crumbs. "You're really going to Richmond?" I asked quietly.

He nodded, his eyes down, frowning into his teacup.

We sat for a few more minutes. "Thanks for the tea," I said softly. I gathered Bit and rose, went to the living room and pulled a book from the shelf. I didn't even notice what it was.

It didn't matter.

Chapter Eleven

I went back to the Town Pharmacy for breakfast after being away for what seemed to be a lifetime. Everyone looked up, frozen, and then began to talk at once.

"We thought you had died," Marie said, "and your body was lying, undiscovered, under a pile of goat poop."

I sat and reached for a coffee mug. Wendy, at least, knew I'd be back, and had set the table as she always had, for the five of us.

"Now, there's an original obituary for you," I said.

"Did you lose your phone?" Marie asked, "or did you just use caller ID to never answer it?"

"I've been...involved," I mumbled.

"You didn't even answer my texts," Karen chided gently.

"Yes, I did. I said I was going through some crap and needed some alone time."

"There's alone time, and then there's self-imposed exile," Stella snapped.

"Able was I, ere I saw Elba," I intoned.

Terri frowned. "What?"

"Elba was where Napoleon spent his last days," Marie explained. "In exile."

"Ah," Terri said. She looked sideways at me. "Well?"

I cleared my throat. "There was drama. With Craig. And now it's over. He and I are nice and civil to each other once again. His ex-father-in-law showed up, and there was a bit of panic there about him stealing the girls, but now it's all good. And Craig got a job in Richmond and he'll be moving at the end of the month."

Stella made a clucking noise. "He should not be disrupting his children again. They have found their place *here*. Why is he moving?"

"Because he can't commute to Richmond. This was always the plan, Stella. He was never going to stay here." I stirred my coffee a bit to aggressively, and some of it spilled. "Never."

"What about Sam's on Main?" Karen asked. "Is he going to sell it? He can't sell it."

"Is it just me?" I asked the air, "or is this deja vu all over again?"

Marie kicked my ankle under the table. "Well?"

I shook my head. "I am out of this, guys. I can't control what happens to Sam's. It's up to Craig and he's not sharing."

Wendy came up, tapping her pencil against her pad. "'Bout time you're back. The usual?"

"Good to see you too, Wendy. I think I'll break with tradition and have an omelet, American cheese. Crispy bacon, crispy potatoes, and multigrain raisin."

She scribbled, looking at me suspiciously. "You okay?"

"Fine, Wendy. Just fine." I spilled more coffee, and pulled a bunch of napkins to sop it up.

"Sure," Wendy said under her breath. "Anyone else breaking with tradition this morning?"

They all shook their heads, and Wendy left, still muttering.

Terri cleared her throat. "The house should be ready next week. We're getting final inspections on Tuesday."

"Oh, that's great," I told her. "Really."

Congratulations ran around the table. Karen even applauded.

Stella's fingers were drumming against the table, her bright red nails practically glowing against her dark skin. "I saw the two of you that night at the pier, Jenna. Do not sit there and tell me you two did not go home and do a little something-something."

"Actually, we did. But that was then. This is now, and now he's moving to Richmond."

"And you?"

I sighed. I had not pursued my plan to grab Kenny Malcolm and renew our brief former relationship. I was so grateful that Craig and I were talking like normal people again I didn't want to start messing up my psyche. "I'm thinking about Boston."

Karen set down her mug so hard we all jumped. "As in *moving* to Boston?"

I shrugged. "Why not? I need a change."

"Then get a haircut," Marie muttered.

"There's snow in Boston," Karen said. "Not like here. *Real* snow. You hate snow."

"And there's no beach there." Terri pointed out. "Well, there is, but you can't go in the water, it's too cold most of the time."

"And *we're* not there," Stella said.

I closed my eyes and put both of my hands, palms down, on the table. "I can't live in that house anymore," I said quietly. "It was bad enough after Sam left. But now..." I had been trying to imagine those empty rooms, the Disney movies gone from the TV stand, my refrigerator once again empty of food.

Terri grabbed my hand and gave it a shake. "Oh, Jenna."

Stella snorted. "Did you *tell* that man that you loved him?"

I nodded. "Yes, Stella, I did, as a matter of fact. He didn't believe me. He thought I was using him as a substitute Sam."

She waved her hand, disgusted. "And is that true?"

"No," I said. "Of course not."

"So," she continued, "did you tell him *that*?"

"Yes!"

Stella shook her head in disgust. "Then I completely fail to see the problem. Unless he is just a pig-headed *man*."

I sighed. "That's the problem."

Wendy arrived and plates passed around. I gazed down. "That

omelet looks just perfect. I mean, look at those edges? Not too brown...and that bacon could be on the cover of *International Bacon Magazine*."

Karen sighed. "Yes. It's a beautiful plate, Jenna. Are you really going to let him leave without trying again?"

I smacked the table with my fist. "Try again how? Tell me. What exactly do I say to a man who has been told that I love him, but he would rather not, thankyouverymuch?"

She was silent. I glared around the table. No suggestions.

"Okay then," I said. "And there it is."

We ate in silence until Karen waved a fork. "I saw Olivia with Kenny Malcolm."

"Now, there's a match made in heaven," Terri said with a grin. "Is he even divorced yet?"

"Did that ever stop her before?" Karen snorted.

I stuffed more omelet into my mouth and munched on a piece of bacon. Well, there went Kenny. Damn.

After breakfast I watched as my friends went their various ways. Karen asked if I would be going back to her yoga class, and I told her probably in the next few weeks. I sat in front of the pharmacy in the sun and watched traffic for a while, then walked down to the beach.

The beach at Cape Edwards isn't like the beach on Seaside, which was what we Eastern Shore people called the Atlantic coast of the peninsula. At low tide, you can walk out for a hundred yards or so, past tidal pools, until you reach actual water. It was crowded, but I took off my shoes and walked out until I hit water, then further until the waves lapped at the bottoms of my shorts. Could I really live in Boston? I'd been to Cape Cod before, and the dunes were beautiful, but I didn't know if I could survive without the sound of the waves and the smell of salt air right outside my bedroom window. But how could I live here now? I'd been young when Sam had broken my heart, and I healed. I'd been a silly girl, swept off my feet. There had been scars, for sure, but I knew that this time, the scars would stay raw and painful for much longer. I loved Craig Ferris in a way I never had Sam. Sam had been my first love.

But Craig, I knew, would be my last love.

Summer may have been winding down, but the weather hadn't given an inch. In the week that followed, the humidity moved in. My clothes stuck to my body just walking from the car to the house. When I made the comment to Craig, he lifted one eyebrow.

"You could always clear out a spot and park in the garage."

"Which means I might have to get rid of things, Craig. Have you even *thought* about that?"

"I've mostly been thinking about why you have so much stuff. Seriously, this is a little beyond just collecting things."

I looked down at my feet. "Things don't...leave." I glanced up. "Every time I open this garage, I know that all this stuff, even if I don't need it anymore, or want it anymore, will still be there. It's...reassuring."

His eyes suddenly filled with something I didn't recognize. Sadness and, what? Pity? I didn't want pity from him.

His mouth twitched. "My mistake. Forget I ever mentioned it."

He heard from Ellis. Robert's new lawyer had talked him out of even trying to get custody. Papers had been filled out, motions had been filed, and then, quite suddenly, everything came to a halt. Robert had driven over from Virginia Beach, rented a boat from the marina and had spent the day with Craig and the girls out in the bay, fishing. Now, he was coming by to say goodbye. He pulled the long Caddy up in front of the house and got out slowly. Penny never left the car.

Robert hugged the girls and shook Craig's hand. "That condo we bought, it would be nice in the winter."

Craig nodded. "That it would. Anything beats Chicago snow."

"Yes, well, if we do drive down, we could stay a few weeks, you know? Spend time with the girls."

"That would be good," Craig said to him. "I know they'd like that."

"And I could let Beverly use it. I always liked Bev. And she misses, well, she'd like to see them too."

"No problem, Rob. Just tell me when."

Rob nodded curtly to me, got in the car, and drove off. Penny, shockingly, did not wave goodbye to me through the passenger side window.

Standing next to Craig, I sighed deeply. "He didn't have a hug for me," I said wistfully.

Craig grinned. "I don't think he was very pleased with you, Jenna. You didn't give him the respect he felt he deserved."

We walked back toward the water. "No, not so much. Who's Bev?"

"His ex-wife," Craig said. "She knew Deb, knew who she really was, and had cut her off, emotionally, years ago. She loved her granddaughters though."

"They're easy to love," I told him. "I'm pretty stuck on them myself."

He glanced at me. "I know that," he said, his voice rough. "And they've grown very attached."

I felt my eyes start to fill with tears. Every time I thought of them leaving, the tears started. For weeks now. I kept telling myself I'd get used to the idea, but so far it still hurt.

Almost as much as it hurt to think about losing Craig.

"It's the goats," I told him. "You may have to get them goats in Richmond."

"It's not the goats," he said. "You've been really good to them." He cleared his throat.

I looked up at him. "They're Sam's grandkids," I said.

He nodded.

"And they're yours. They are part of who you are, and that makes them even more important to me than I could have ever thought possible."

"Is that why you stood up to Robert that day? Because that was really something. I'll never forget you for that."

"You mean otherwise, you *would* forget me?"

He stopped so suddenly that I took few steps past him. When I turned, there were tears in his eyes.

"Craig?"

"How could I possibly?" he asked, his voice shaking. "After all you've done? You saved me, Jenna. You saved *us*."

"I did what I did for *you*. I would have done anything for you, Craig. Anything." My own voice was very clear and steady. I clenched my fists. This was my chance. I could see it, right in front of me. Maybe I couldn't keep him. Maybe, no matter what I said, he'd leave. But at least, if he did, I would have given us my best shot.

"I know you didn't believe me the first time I said it, but I love you. And it's not because of Sam, and it's not because I'm lonely and it's not because I had an itch that needed to be scratched." I stepped toward him. "I don't want to be dazzled. I don't want someone to sweep me off my feet like Sam did. I'm all grown up now and I know what's important. I know what's real, and what is going to last. And I know that I want you."

He put his hands up and pressed the palms of his hands against his eyes. When he dropped them, his eyes were clear.

"I love you, too, Jenna."

My heart jumped into my throat. He just said that he loved me. Finally, the words were there, right in front of me, and I could see in his face he meant them. He loved me, and there came such a rush of happiness that I couldn't breathe.

But...It couldn't be that easy. There would be a *but*. But he'd already sold the restaurant, but the job in Richmond was too much money to pass up, but, but, but...

"From the very beginning." The words were tumbling out of him so fast I had to lean in to catch every one. "You made me crazy, you know that? With your dogs barking and your ridiculous goats, and running around half naked. And can we talk just a minute about all your stuff, just, well, *everywhere?* That garden of yours? Do you really need to smell like compost all the time? And Sam...you were so in love with him. How was I supposed to compete with a ghost?" He paused to take a deep breath, and I jumped in.

"I was only half naked that one time."

He shook his head. "One time was enough." He grabbed me by the shoulders. "I don't know how he didn't tell me about you. If I had a woman like you in my life, I would have told the whole world."

I flew at him, both fists raised, and hit him, hard, pounding my fists against his chest. "I could kill you, Craig Ferris. Why the hell didn't you say so?"

He grabbed both of my wrists and held them. "You were my father's wife, Jenna. His wife. We never knew each other, but the two of you, together...it made my feelings for you all that much harder to figure out. It made me wanting you seem..."

I nodded. "Yeah, I had to think about that too. But you and I, Craig, we belonged together. Sam was a part of our lives, but never a part of *us*, together. Didn't you see that?"

"I was afraid," he said. "After Sam, I was afraid I'd let you down. That I wouldn't be enough."

"You are an idiot. I *told* you I loved you. I told you that it was *you* I wanted, not some ghost. Why didn't you just believe me the first time? Or even the third time? Am I going to have to spend the rest of my life telling you how much I love you?"

He clenched his jaw. "God, I hope so," he muttered, and kissed me.

He let go of my wrists and they hung, limply at my sides, as I just leaned up against him, my mouth on his, while around me the world jumped and whirled and spun from pure happiness.

I wrapped my arms around his neck and pulled him closer. I could feel the long, lean lines of his body. I knew what they would feel like against me, how his skin would taste, how the gentle strength in his hands would move across my back and down.

More than all that, I felt perfect and complete, as though every single moment of my life had been leading to just this.

I heard Finn barking. I didn't care. And then I heard laughter, little girls' laughter, and I started laughing too, my mouth still against his, because in one moment, everything had changed.

"Why are you kissing?"

"That's gross."

"No, it's not gross."

"Do you like kissing?"

"Does this mean you're going to stop being Grandma?"

I pushed Craig away and dropped to my knees, taking them both in my arms. "Yes, you, I'm finally going to stop being your grandma."

Chris threw a little party on a Sunday afternoon to show off her new house, and even though the season had barely started winding down, Craig took off work to come with me. It was our first official appearance in Cape Edwards as a couple, and I was feeling pretty good about the whole thing. I not only wore a long, pretty sundress, I put on mascara.

The house was a marvel. Yes, they'd put in new floors, but not a new ceiling, and the whole space was vaulted, like a cathedral, with tiny, high windows at the eaves, letting in even more light.

Both the McCann brothers were in attendance. It looked like Terri somehow got her man. She was calm and subtle about it, holding her hand up, and pointing the finger of her other hand in his direction, mouthing, "mine."

Stella and Dara French came late. So did Kenny Malcolm and Olivia. She greeted Craig with a kiss on both cheeks while completely ignoring me. I watched her for a bit until she was off by herself, pouring a glass of wine.

I sidled up beside her. "So, you and Kenny? Somehow, that makes sense," I said.

She arched an eyebrow. "Really? How nice of you to say that, Jenna. Now, about you and Craig..."

I leaned toward her and she actually shrank back. "Craig and I are fine. We were always fine, no matter what kind of trash you had to say about us. Keep your mouth shut, Olivia. You're not the only one with dirty laundry. And I can be just as big a bitch as you can, so don't test me. Got it?"

She looked at me steadily. "Yes. I've got it. Keep your Craig Ferris, Jenna. I hope you're happy with him." Then she drank off her wine in one gulp and walked back to the party.

Chris cornered me on her front porch, her eyes dancing. "I'm glad to see you so happy, Jenna. Craig is so great. You and he...fit together."

I smiled. "Yes, as a matter of fact, we do. Now, what about you and Mike McCann?"

She grinned. "We're exploring possibilities."

"That's good. That's very good. Mike seems a good guy."

"He is. I'm not so sure about his brother." She made a face. "I think Terri is going to end up disappointed."

"Terri is a big girl," I told her. "She knows what she's getting herself into."

Chris sighed happily. "I guess. My only regret is that I never had a chance to have breakfast with all you single ladies."

I thought. "I can't imagine giving them up," I said slowly. "We may have to expand our breakfast club requirements to include the newly deliriously attached."

She laughed. "Deliriously attached? I love that! Yes, I think I'd fit right in."

I looked past her as Craig came out on the porch. He put his arm around my shoulder and I leaned against him.

Happiness complete.

Craig moved into my bedroom right away, and offered his empty room to one of the twins, but they refused to be separated.

"I don't like sleeping alone."

"That room is really small."

"And there's a creepy noise at night."

"That's just the wind."

"But it never got painted."

"And the floor is yucky."

School started, and he declined the job in Richmond. He also decided to sell the restaurant to Glory. They worked out a deal that split the whole of Sam's on Main into two separate legal entities. He would no longer work at the bar, but continue to own it. She would pay him in monthly installments for the restaurant half.

I looked at him critically. "And what, exactly, are you going to *do* all day, if you're not working at the bar? 'Cause all that money won't last forever, and I don't want you getting fat and lazy and ruining that great butt of yours."

He raised his eyebrows. "Great butt?"

I cocked my head at him. "You don't think I love you just for your mind, do you?"

He chuckled and shook his head. "The number of businesses on Main Street that don't have a website is shocking. Do you know you can't even access the menu at Treacher's online? I'm going into business for myself, web development and hosting, and I'm going to use Sam's old apartment as my office."

"Well, that will be convenient, having your customers come up right through the bar."

He grinned and tapped his index finger to his forehead. "Always thinking, Jenna. Always thinking." He looked at me, and an odd look came over his face. "I'm not the one who should be worrying about gaining weight. Have you noticed lately that you actually have boobs?"

"You're complaining?"

"No. I'm just wondering about that night out here in the back. You know, when I didn't use a condom. That was, what, two months ago?"

We were sitting in the dock, watching the fish swim, listening to the girls playing with the dogs. I stared down into the water, thinking fast. Oh, dear Lord...

"Jenna?"

I looked at him, my whole body tense with a mixture of fear and excitement. "Oh, God, Craig, what if I *am* pregnant?"

He burst into laughter. "That would be pretty wonderful."

"But...I'm old."

"Not that old."

"But Sam and I tried. I mean, we really *tried*..."

His arm went around me and I felt his mouth in my hair. "Sometimes, it's just the right combination. And you and I, well, let's face it. We're a pretty spectacular pair."

"I'd have to quit my job." My mind was racing so fast I felt dizzy just sitting there.

"Not forever. Not if you didn't want to. I could be a househusband. I already do the cooking, and the cleaning, not to mention..."

"Craig," I yelled. "This is serious."

He looked at me, the smile gone, but his eyes glowing. "Yes, Jenna. You're right. This *is* serious. And I am seriously thrilled to death at the thought of you and I having a child together. You're already a terrific mom, and I cannot wait to see you with this baby."

I could not for the life of me single out one of the thousand things I had on the tip of my tongue to actually say. I opened my mouth, but absolutely nothing came out

"Jenna, don't tell me you're speechless?"

"If it's a boy, we have to name him Sam. Or a girl. Either way. We just have to."

He took my face between his hands and kissed me.

"True that."

And that's what we did.

A quick look at the next Eastern Shore
Romance...

❧

Building Home

I'd never been much of a risk taker.

I was a good girl in high school. I dated a nice, quiet boy, a few years older than I, who invariably apologized after we had sex because I didn't scream out loud when I had an orgasm. It wasn't his fault, because, although I never told him, I never really *had* an orgasm, despite all his efforts. He was such a great guy that I didn't want to disappoint him. Maybe if I had offered a suggestion or two, or maybe even moved his hand to the right spot, things would have worked out differently. But, like I said, I didn't take risks, and I was not going to seem pushy or sexually aggressive because he might break up with me, and *then* where would I be?

That was my life. My whole life. Lots of things happened between then and now, but...

Now I stood, gazing at my cell phone, and at pictures of a rather dilapidated house that my old college roommate was trying to talk me into.

Buy it, she said.

It's a great investment, she said.

It's right on Main Street in Cape Edwards, and you can walk to all the bars and restaurants, as well as the beach, she said.

You could open a real estate office right in town.

Or do something completely different.

Or take the money from your mom's estate and just be a lady of leisure.

You could start your life all over.

Begin a new second act.

And you've been here before and you always say you love it. And do you remember all the hot men?

I didn't, actually. And, to be honest, hot men were not a priority. Over a year ago I'd broken up with Daniel, my boyfriend of eleven years, to care for my mother. I discovered that my life hummed along just fine without him in it. Based on that, I pretty much decided that if being unattached for the rest of my natural life was going to be a thing, it was NOT going to be the end of the world.

I flipped through the pictures again. It was a cute little house, just two bedrooms, with a wide front porch. Inside, walls were sagging and the kitchen was impossible. There wasn't a picture of the bathroom, which I knew was not a very good sign. But it was all workable. Even the sad looking little backyard had great potential, with some pavers and a few potted plants. I could have a dog. I'd never had a dog before: my first husband was a cat person, Daniel had been allergic, and I had spent most of the past two years spending all my non-working hours caring for my mother, slowly wasting away from cancer, which left no time to devote to a pet. Or for Daniel, come to that.

I'd been selling houses in Rehoboth, Delaware for almost twenty-five years, and I was good at it. But I had never owned my own home. When I married Martin, my first husband, I moved into his condo right from my parents' house. After the divorce, I went back to Mom's. Then, I moved in with Daniel. Then, I moved back in with Mom after she got sick.

Finally, my own house.

Right on Main Street.

Close to bars and restaurants.

With all those hot men...

Why the hell not?

I thought about it for almost a month, during which time I settled my mother's estate and tried to find a way to live comfortably in *her* house.

I couldn't. It would always be her house, not mine.

I finally did the work and realized how much it was worth.

Holy crap.

I looked at those pictures again. It was selling for dirt cheap because the interior needed so much work, like a brand new kitchen and bathroom, paint... a major rehab job. Terri, in her original text had mentioned something about the perfect guys to help with the renovation, and how we could flip the property and become HGTV stars.

Terri got carried away with some of her ideas, but if she already knew who to help with the renovation...

Sold! I texted her.

Terri's return text was a series of emojis. Then, of course, she called.

"Oh, Chris, this is going to be so much fun! You can stay with me and we can walk to the job site every day."

"Terri," I warned her, "you have somebody to do the renovations, right?"

"Yes. The McCann brothers. Steve McCann and I have, if I can brag just a little, a certain chemistry. I know that once he and I start working together, things will really start to take off. He's a bit younger than I am, but that's fine. What's a five year difference at our age?""

"So...you want me to buy this house so you can hit on some *guy*?"

"Of course not. I want you to buy this house because every time you've come down here, you've had a great time."

That was true.

"And you've had a rough couple of years with your mom. You've lived in the same place your whole life, Chris. and could use a change of scenery."

That was also true.

"Change is good for the soul. Don't you feel like you need to shake things up? Now is your chance."

I sighed. "You're right. Let's do this. I guess I can drive down there for the sale, but I have to close the office up here, and that's going to take a while. Can you buy this for me?"

"Of course."

"OK then. I'll send you a Power of Attorney, wire you the cash, and we can get going."

She squealed. Fifty-year-old women should not squeal, but that's Terri for you.

"Oh, Chris, I am so excited. And you know what the best part is?"

I was smiling over the phone. "That you and I will be able to walk to each other's houses every day?"

"No, I meant, beside that. Steve McCann has a older brother. His name is Mike, and he has a beard, and he's closer to our age, and I know the two of you would be perfect together." She clicked off the phone before I could yell WTF?

As a point of information, I eventually married that nice, quiet high school boy, and I eventually had an orgasm. But not with him.

Order Building Home Now!